A Token
of Truth

A Token of Truth

SUNNI JEFFERS

GUIDEPOSTS
NEW YORK, NEW YORK

www.guideposts.com
(800) 431-2344
Guideposts Books & Inspirational Media

Cover design by Dugan Design Group
Cover illustration by Rose Lowry, www.illustrations.com
Interior design by Cris Kossow
Typeset by Nancy Tardi
Printed in the United States of America

For Beth Adams, with my deepest gratitude and admiration. You're amazing. You always encourage me and exercise such patience. You are a joy, and I'm privileged to call you friend. Thank you.

To all the readers who follow Kate and Paul's stories, thank you for coming along on this journey. May your lives be filled with the joy and wonder and mysteries of God's marvelous world.

Chapter One

Kate Hanlon slammed her foot on the brake, sending the Honda's rear tires sliding on a glaze of ice. Her heartbeat shot into overdrive as a hulking blue wreck of a truck, spewing exhaust, shot across the road in front of her. Pain shot through her wrists and up her arms as she gripped the steering wheel and held on for dear life.

The tires grabbed pavement, jerking the car to a stop in the middle of the road. *If there'd been traffic . . .* She inhaled deeply. *But there wasn't.* She released her breath.

The other driver had peeled out of the Quik Stop on the corner of Mountain Laurel Road and Sweetwater. Kate had come to a stop facing her turn onto Sweetwater. Would she ever be comfortable driving on icy roads? All her years of driving hadn't prepared her for winters in the mountains of Eastern Tennessee.

A plume of black exhaust puffed out in billowy clouds, trailing the blue truck all the way up Sweetwater Street. It had all happened so fast; only seconds had passed. A flash of irritation rippled through Kate. *Where is Deputy Spencer when you need him?* Her jaws hurt from clenching her teeth. She took another deep breath, then exhaled slowly, letting out her tension. She was in one piece. Her car hadn't hit anything —or anyone. *Thank you, Lord!*

Her back tires skidded on the slick surface, then caught as she accelerated gingerly. She headed up Sweetwater, hoping the smog machine ahead of her would keep going straight. If the driver turned onto Pine Ridge Road, it would take them over the steep grade, and she didn't want to choke on his exhaust all the way to Pine Ridge.

She'd nearly caught up to the truck when it slowed and careened to the left, taking up the middle of the road, barely missing a minivan coming toward it. As the truck angled into the turn, giving her a glimpse of the driver, Kate did a double take.

Skip Spencer?

It couldn't be! The truck swung wide, barely missing the guardrail before straightening out.

She followed the truck onto Pine Ridge Road. What would Copper Mill's deputy be doing driving a smoke machine, weaving all over the road like that on a Thursday morning?

It couldn't be him. But she'd seen his distinctive red hair. It *had* to be the young deputy.

The truck veered right, then left, as if running a defensive zigzag pattern. Why, Kate couldn't imagine. The rear passenger-side tire wobbled. She kept a safe distance behind and hoped it wouldn't fall off.

Skip crossed the dividing line again as he sped around a

corner. A delivery van honked at him, and he moved over just in time. Kate was afraid that if he didn't run himself off the road, he would send someone else into a ditch.

At a straightaway near the summit, the road widened, with a passing lane. Kate could see ahead almost half a mile before the next turn. Not a car in sight, and the road looked dry.

Pulling around the ancient pickup, Kate honked and waved at Skip as she came alongside. He glanced over, frowning. Then surprise registered on his face. He motioned for her to fall back. Instead, she surged ahead.

Edging around in front of him, she slowed just before the road narrowed to one lane and they reached the next hairpin curve, forcing Skip to slow down behind her.

Just beyond the curve, there was a pullout. Waving and pointing toward the side of the road, Kate slowed more. A line of cars coming at them prevented Skip from roaring around her. He pulled off the road, jerked to a stop, and jumped out of the truck. Kate put her car in park, set the emergency brake, and got out.

"W-what do you think you're doing, Missus Hanlon?" he demanded, his deep voice rising. He ran his fingers through his hair, and his dark hazel eyes blazed. "You could've got us both killed."

"*Me?*"

A frigid wind raced up the chasm between the hills, buffeting Kate and blowing her hair away from her face. She was glad she'd worn the fleece-lined gloves Paul had given her for Christmas. This winter she needed them, but the same didn't seem to be true for Skip. He had on a plaid flannel shirt, jeans, and work boots. No hat. No gloves. Not even a jacket. She put her hands on her hips.

"I was worried about you. You pulled right out in front of me back at the Quik Stop, and you've been weaving all over the road. Your back tire is shaking like it's going to fall off, and your tailpipe is turning red."

"Yeah, uh, sorry 'bout that. Didn't see you." He scratched his head and looked away.

Kate thought he seemed nervous. Skip was a nice young man and enthusiastic about his work, but he tended to plow headlong into trouble at times.

"You'd better go to the auto-repair shop and have your steering adjusted and your tires balanced before you run off the road," Kate said.

"I can't. I've got to go." He started backing away toward his truck. "I'm sorry."

He opened the truck door and looked directly at her. "You drive careful and don't go passing any more cars. I'd hate to have to give you a ticket for reckless driving." He jumped into the cab, gunned the motor, ground it into gear, and took off, spewing exhaust, leaving Kate coughing and sputtering.

She stared at the disappearing vehicle, flabbergasted. Since moving to Copper Mill, Kate had helped Skip solve numerous mysteries, and he'd always expressed gratitude. She knew he respected her, and she respected him too. What the young man lacked in wisdom and experience, he made up for with zeal and a desire to help others, qualities Kate valued.

Kate looked up at the icy blue January sky. "Lord, I hope you're riding along with him, because I think he needs help," she said out loud. "Please keep him safe and get him where he's going, and keep everyone else on the road safe too. I don't know what's bothering him, but there's something wrong."

KATE'S ERRANDS IN PINE RIDGE took longer than she'd expected. She stopped first at the nursing home where she spent over an hour with sweet old Violet Hicks, a woman from Faith Briar Church, where Kate's husband, Paul, was the pastor.

Kate had brought a stained-glass sun catcher that she'd made. When she attached it to the window in Violet's room, the tears in the older woman's eyes told Kate the ornament was a hit.

A stroke had left Violet partially paralyzed, but she grunted and stuttered, finally forming the words "thank you."

Kate scooted a chair close to the bed and patiently conversed with the elderly lady until her eyes began to close. She was asleep when Kate left.

Kate grabbed a bite of lunch at the SuperMart, then zipped through her list of errands. Paul had asked her to pick up a few things at the hardware store, which took much longer than she'd expected. She couldn't believe how many different kinds and sizes of screws there were, not to mention the variety of track lighting fixtures.

A nice young man helped her find the items Paul needed. By the time she left the store and loaded her purchases in the trunk, the sun was peeking through the thinning clouds. The wind had abated, and all signs of frost had disappeared. She removed her gloves and stuffed them into her pocket.

As Kate climbed into her car and headed back toward Pine

Ridge Road, she prayed that Skip had reached his destination safely. Spotting the top of the Harrington County Courthouse through the barren trees, she made a quick turn and headed toward the building. The white Grecian columns and thin Federalist-style windows of the historical, antebellum building faced the Pine Ridge town square.

Inside, as Kate reached for the door to the auditor's office, it jerked open, and Sheriff Roberts nearly mowed her down. He stepped back.

"Kate. How are you?"

"Hello, Sheriff. I'm glad I ran into you. I'm concerned about Skip."

"What has that deputy done now?" he asked as they moved into the hall to get out of the doorway.

"Well, Skip was driving to Pine Ridge this morning in an old pickup truck. I thought he was on duty."

"He is. He should be on duty now," the sheriff affirmed.

"I flagged him down because his back tire was wobbly, and he seemed to be having trouble with his steering. He pulled off the road, and I got out to tell him about his tire. He seemed quite agitated. I've never seen him speed or drive erratically. He assured me that his truck was all right, then he drove off in a big hurry." Kate neglected to mention that Skip almost ran her down coming out of the Quik Stop. She didn't want to get him into more trouble.

"I assumed he was on duty and on police business, but he wasn't in uniform," Kate said. "It didn't seem right. Is he working undercover?"

"Not that I'm aware of. What time was this?"

"About ten thirty." Kate shoved her hands into her pockets.

The sheriff frowned. "Driving a personal vehicle on duty is against policy. I wouldn't approve that, even in an emergency. Too much liability." His jaw tightened. "I'll look into it as soon as I finish up a few things here. Rest assured, Kate, I'll speak to him." He gave her a brief nod. "Thanks for reporting this."

"Yes, of course, you're welcome," she said, frowning as he stepped away. She watched him walk down the hall, his steps heavy. Kate had witnessed the sheriff's exasperation with his deputy before and hated to fuel his shaky opinion of Skip. She hadn't reported the incident to tattle on Skip. She hoped she hadn't gotten him in trouble, but something told her there was more involved in the odd episode than Skip's erratic driving.

By THE TIME Kate headed back home, it was three o'clock. She decided to stop in at the Copper Mill Town Hall to see if Skip had gotten back safely.

As she climbed the concrete steps to the austere two-story, red-brick building, a tall, reed-thin man came through the doors wearing heavy work boots and a green wool jacket. He stopped and held the door open for her.

"Good afternoon, ma'am," he said, his words clipped. He touched the brim of his hat with a folded tourist brochure. His leathery skin crinkled like old parchment when he smiled.

Kate returned his smile. "Thank you."

"You're welcome." He stood aside so she could enter. "Have a nice afternoon."

"You too. Thanks."

Kate caught a slightly sweet, earthy scent as she passed him and entered the lobby of the building. Across from the doorway, a large glass display case held a few artifacts from the copper mines that once flourished in the area. A faded picture and newspaper clipping outlined the history of the Old Copper Road, which enabled miners to transport ore out of the mountains, and another newspaper article showed a commemorative coin, front and back. The picture was poor, but the coin had the mine's name and a loaded mine cart on one side and a caravan of ore wagons on the Old Copper Road on the other side. The coin itself was the centerpiece of the display, mounted in the center of a round, slightly faded, green velvet background.

When Kate and Paul had first moved to town, the mayor had proudly shown them the case and told them about the precious commemorative coin.

The lobby was empty as Kate walked through. With barely a glance, she turned to the right and entered the small deputy's office.

The front desk that Skip normally occupied was vacant.

"Hello," Kate called out. No one answered.

She walked to the double doors leading to the jail cells and knocked. She waited, but no one came. She checked to see if Skip had left a note saying when he'd be back.

The only thing Kate noticed was a sign-in clipboard on the desk, which had several names listed for that day. At a quick glance, she noticed two names with contact addresses listed as rooms at the Hamilton Springs Hotel. One requested permission to enter a restricted area at the old copper mine, and the last entry requested information on the regulations for gathering ore samples as souvenirs. From the time notation next to the name, Kate assumed this visitor—Griff Henley— must have been the man who held the door for her.

It'd been five hours since Kate had seen Skip. She'd hoped he'd be back at his desk. Seeing no sign of him, Kate turned to leave but paused when the telephone rang. After a couple of rings, the answering machine clicked on.

A brief message gave instructions to call 911 in an emergency, then a voice came through. It was the sheriff. On impulse, Kate picked up the phone.

"Sheriff Roberts, this is Kate Hanlon."

"Kate, why are you picking up the phone? Give me Deputy Spencer."

"Well, he isn't here. No one is. Is everything all right?"

"That's what I'd like to know. He knows not to leave prisoners unattended for so long. I'll send a Harrington County deputy over there right away."

"Wait. I knocked on the door to the cells, and no one answered. Hold on a minute."

Kate saw several sets of keys on a hook behind the door. She'd seen Skip retrieve the keys to the jail cells when she'd come to visit prisoners before. On top was a set of car keys. *Skip's county SUV*, she wondered, since he hadn't been driving it. She took the jail keys, replacing the others, and went over to the double doors. She knocked again. When no one responded, she unlocked the door and peeked inside. Both cells were empty. She returned to the phone:

"Sheriff, there aren't any prisoners in the cells."

"What?"

Kate held the phone away from her ear as he blasted his question. She could almost hear his teeth grinding.

"Maybe someone posted bail?" she suggested tentatively, trying to smooth over the matter.

"Not through my office. I'm coming over myself. The man isn't dangerous, and he can't have gone far, but he's failed to appear before. I need to find him. Go on home. I'll look into this."

"Yes, sir."

Kate wondered about this odd turn of events. Maybe Skip was chasing the escapee. Then she came along and delayed him. That still didn't answer why he was driving an old truck, though.

As Kate walked back through the Town Hall to leave, she glanced at the glass display case. Something about the display looked different. She stepped closer.

The newspaper articles were there, as were the old photos of the mines. Her eyes shifted to the coin.

She blinked and peered closer. It wasn't the valued coin. It wasn't a coin at all. It was a token for a free car wash at a highway truck stop. Someone had stolen the Copper Mill commemorative coin!

Chapter Two

Kate hated to jump to conclusions. There might be a perfectly logical explanation for the coin exchange. Someone could have removed it for cleaning or something equally innocent. But the replacement struck her as odd, almost sacrilegious. The town held the coin in high regard as a token of its historical legacy.

Kate turned and headed back down the hall toward the mayor's office. Mayor Briddle would know why there'd been a switch. When she entered, a tall woman with wavy gray hair turned from the metal filing cabinet to face her. Kate recognized Clara Briddle, the mayor's aunt, who'd recently retired from teaching at Copper Mill High School. The school had held an open house to honor her forty years of teaching in Copper Mill.

Clara peered over the top of her glasses at Kate. She removed the glasses and let them drop to dangle from the silver chain around her neck.

"Good afternoon, Mrs. Hanlon. How may I help you?"

she asked, raising her eyebrows as she came to the counter separating the office area from the entry.

Kate had met Clara on several occasions and knew her formality was engrained in her personality. She had taught several generations of Copper Mill students, running her classroom with a firm hand and a solid oak ruler.

"I didn't realize you worked for the mayor now."

"Oh yes. When I saw the condition of my nephew's files, I volunteered to reorganize the office for him. He's so busy, and I have time on my hands. I don't know why he didn't replace his secretary when she moved away two years ago." She placed her hands on the counter. "But now he doesn't need to. He has me for free."

"How fortunate for him and for Copper Mill," Kate said with a polite smile. "Say, do you know if anyone has redone the lobby display case?"

"No." Clara shook her head. "No one touches that case without permission. Even the cleaning lady has to check out the key from the deputy's office." She paused, then cleared her throat. "As far as I know, the case hasn't been opened other than for cleaning for some time."

"When was the cleaning lady here last?"

"Tuesday." Clara crossed her arms over her chest. "Gertie always cleans on Tuesday."

"Gertie?"

"Gertie Crowe. She's been cleaning Town Hall for years." Clara narrowed her eyes at Kate. "Why do you ask?"

"Well, the coin in the case is different. It's ..."

Clara's eyes widened, and before Kate could finish, the

older woman came around the counter and marched out the door.

"I was wondering who's been to Town Hall since it was cleaned . . . ," Kate said, hurrying down the hallway after her.

Clara waved her hand dismissively. "Half the town. Fred Cowan was in. Lucy Mae had a meeting in the multipurpose room with Renee Lambert and Patricia Harris and some others to plan the Saint Patrick's Day Parade. Arlene Jacobs has an exercise class there on Wednesday mornings."

Clara came to an abrupt halt in front of the display, leaned toward the glass, then gasped. "What in the world?" She blinked and looked closer. "Why, it's impossible."

"Then the coin wasn't removed for cleaning or appraisal, perhaps?" Kate suggested.

"No one is authorized to remove that coin." Clara put on her glasses and leaned closer, as if it might change what she was seeing. "Not without the deputy's approval. When did this happen?"

"I don't know. I came by to see Deputy Spencer a little while ago, and I noticed the coin had been replaced with this token."

"Skip Spencer better have a good explanation for this," Clara straightened and made a low sound under her breath. "Why they would put a feckless young man in charge of a valuable historical treasure, I'll never know. That coin is irreplaceable!" She turned and marched into the deputy's office.

"Oh, the deputy isn't there," Kate called after her, following her again. "I know it's old, but is the coin valuable? It isn't an actual coin, is it?"

"Is it valuable?" Clara repeated, her voice a near shriek. "It's priceless!" She jerked the office door back and looked behind it for the key. She rifled through several jangling sets before she found the cabinet key on the bottom of the stack. "There it is. The scoundrel returned the key!"

"Are you sure?" Kate peered at the shiny brass piece of metal. It could be a key to anything.

"I'm sure." Clara gave Kate a withering look.

Kate stepped back.

"Now what thief would take the time to return the key?" Clara said. "It has to be an inside job. Call Sheriff Roberts."

"I just spoke with him a few minutes ago," Kate said. "I believe he's on his way here now."

"This can't wait. I can't believe . . . I've known Skip since he was a tyke, and he doesn't have a lick of sense, but I've never known him to break the law."

She touched a finger to her chin. "Though now that I think about it, I recall coming upon him staring at the coin the other day. Where is that boy?"

"I don't know. I saw him this morning on my way to Pine Ridge. I thought he'd be back by now."

Clara's eyes grew wide. "My goodness. He's absconded with it. We'll never see the likes of him again, mark my words."

She grabbed the telephone receiver off Skip's desk and punched in three numbers. "That coin must be worth a fortune. His poor mother must be beside herself with worry and remorse. Spare the rod and spoil the child, you know."

Kate didn't have to guess that she was calling 911, and she couldn't help but think that Clara was being just a bit melodramatic.

Clara turned her back on Kate and began reporting a theft, explaining to the emergency dispatcher how she discovered the missing coin.

"The deputy, he's the one who stole it," Clara said emphatically. "You'd better put out an APB."

Clara was being far too accusatory, but Kate supposed she could understand why the woman would jump to the conclusion that Skip was guilty. He did have the access and time to take the coin. But why would he? What possible reason would he have to bring disgrace to the badge he wore so proudly?

Kate decided to have another look at the case. On the way out of the deputy's office, she noticed a residue of dried footprints on the floor in front of Skip's desk. The prints were large, and she could make out the distinct pattern of heavy-tread work boots.

Kate returned to the lobby and leaned in to get a good look inside the case. The copper token looked dull, probably from being handled by many dirty fingers. She wondered if that might make it difficult to get a good set of prints from it. She recognized the logo of a truck stop with a tractor-trailer rig on the front. She and Paul had stopped for gas at the chain of truck stops along the interstate.

From what Kate could tell, the lock on the case had no scratches or pry marks on it. It seemed clear that someone must have used the key and replaced it. She noted the same distinctive tread marks on the floor and traces of a fine white powdery substance, like chalk dust from a blackboard.

Kate had no idea how the coin disappeared or who might have taken it, but she wanted to believe in Skip's innocence.

His rush out of town could have been pure coincidence. Her mind whirled with possibilities as she drove home.

The sheriff had mentioned a prisoner. Perhaps the prisoner escaped from jail and stole the coin. Sheriff Roberts had said the prisoner wasn't dangerous, but a theft could have changed things. If the coin was valuable, the perpetrator could be desperate. Skip may have been chasing that very escapee . . . and she'd delayed him. She hoped she hadn't unwittingly aided a jailbreak. Poor Skip was in enough trouble without her help.

Chapter Three

Kate shrugged off her coat and hung it on the coat tree by the front door, pondering whether to warm up leftover lasagna or quick-defrost chicken breasts in the microwave. Neither choice appealed to her.

She heard Paul's footsteps behind her just before his arms came around her. She leaned back into his hug.

"Hi." She let his warmth envelop her. Her shoulders relaxed.

"Hi, yourself." He planted a light kiss on her neck. "Thanks for running my errands today."

"You're welcome."

"Have you planned dinner yet?"

"No. I thought we might have leftovers," she said, resigned to rewarming the previous night's meal. It had been very good, but right now it didn't inspire much enthusiasm.

"I have a better idea. Let me take you out. You've been running errands all day, so it's the least I can do. Besides, the Country Diner is serving roasted chicken with all the trimmings tonight."

Kate's stomach began to growl. She laughed.

"I knew that would entice you," Paul said.

Kate turned and smiled up at her husband. The tiny lines around his clear-blue eyes crinkled as he looked at her. He leaned down and kissed her.

"*Mmm*. You're right," she said. "I am hungry. Just let me wash up, and I'll be ready."

"I'll warm up the car. It's getting colder outside."

"That's an understatement," Kate said as she started across the large living room toward their bedroom. "I skidded on ice this morning."

"Kate?"

She saw Paul's frown and hurried faster. "No dents in the car. I'll tell you about it on the way," she said over her shoulder.

TWENTY MINUTES LATER, after they'd sat at the curb with the motor running and the windows fogging up while Kate recounted the events of her day, Paul turned off the car. They entered the crowded diner and found an empty table near the back. A young waitress was wiping down the table when they approached. She stepped back.

"Good evening," Paul said to her as he helped Kate remove her coat, then held her chair for her while she sat down. "Smells great in here."

"That's our special. It's delicious," the young woman said.

Kate wondered where LuAnne was for the evening. Sometimes, when the diner was extraordinarily busy or when LuAnne needed a day off, various waitresses would fill in for her.

Kate didn't know this waitress, and she would have surely remembered someone with such interesting taste in clothing. The young woman wore a long broomstick skirt, a white T-shirt, several strands of colorful beads with a large amber cabochon wrapped in filigreed copper wire. Her long curly hair was pulled back and wrapped in an orange scarf. She caught Kate staring at her necklace and smiled.

"My name's Sheena Perry." She held out her hand. "We just moved here."

"I'm Kate Hanlon," she said, shaking Sheena's hand, "and this is my husband, Paul." She gestured toward him. "Welcome to Copper Mill. We're fairly new here too. And I love your necklace."

"Thanks. I made it myself." She shrugged. "I'll get you some water and give you a chance to look at the menu." She turned, her skirt swinging gracefully, and left them.

Kate looked over the menu, even though she knew it by heart.

Sheena returned a few minutes later with water and set glasses in front of them. "Are you ready to order?" she asked, taking out a pad and pencil.

"I've decided to have the catfish, and please substitute a salad for the hush puppies," Kate said.

"I'll have the roasted half-chicken dinner," Paul ordered. He looked at Kate and winked.

She raised her eyebrows but didn't comment. He was supposed to watch his cholesterol, but what could she say? He was a grown man. Besides, the roasting process was supposed to leave less fat than traditional fried chicken.

"You won't be sorry," Sheena said. "I hope there's some left tonight. Loretta said I could take some home to Tom if there's any left."

Kate glanced at Paul. She could see his indecision and knew he was wondering whether to change his order so Tom could have the chicken. Sheena must have noticed too. She held up a hand, as if to stop him.

"There's lots of chicken back there," she said. "Loretta said she had enough to feed the whole town."

Paul smiled and relaxed.

Kate noticed a simple wedding band on Sheena's finger. "Is Tom your husband?"

"Yeah." She held up her hand and wiggled her ring finger. "Three months tomorrow."

"Congratulations," Kate said. "How long have you been in Copper Mill?"

"Two weeks. Tom wants to get settled and start a business so we can raise a family in a small town." She blushed. "First he's got to find some work. Do you know anyone who needs a carpenter or a handyman? He's really good."

"I don't know of anything right offhand, but I'd like to meet him," Paul said. "I could introduce him to some of the people in town."

"That'd be super, Mr. Hanlon. I'll tell him. How can he reach you?"

Paul pulled a business card out of his pocket and handed it to her. Her eyes widened. She looked at Paul. "Oh, wow. You're a minister."

He nodded and gave her a smile.

"If you haven't found a church home, we'd love to have you visit ours," Kate said. "We have several young married couples."

"We're pretty busy on Sundays, but I'll tell Tom," Sheena said. "I'll go turn in your order."

The young waitress hurried away. Kate hoped she hadn't said something to upset her. She gave Paul a helpless look. He patted her hand. They both knew what it was like to move to a small town—especially this small town. People were friendly and caring, but sometimes it took a while to break the ice.

Knowing Paul, he was already planning to find out where the couple lived and visit Tom to welcome him to town. She would bake a fresh batch of chocolate-chip cookies for Paul to take along. What man could resist them?

A group came into the diner. Kate recognized the man she'd seen at Town Hall that afternoon. A short, plump woman stood beside him, talking to him. Several people stood behind them.

Sheena went to greet them, spoke with the short woman, then went to clear off a vacated table. J. B. Packer, the part-time cook, came out of the kitchen to help her, and they pushed two tables together.

Paul turned to see what Kate was looking at, then turned back to her. "I don't recognize them. Do you?"

"I saw the tall man today when I stopped by Town Hall. That was right before I noticed the old commemorative coin was missing."

Paul frowned. "Just don't you go chasing crooks, especially on these icy roads. I hear we're in for more snow. Clifton Beasley was complaining this morning that it's too cold to sit outside the Mercantile. He says we haven't had a winter this cold in twenty years."

"He would know. Too bad he and his cronies weren't outside today. They might have seen if anyone strange was hanging around town." She took a sip of her water. "But someone must have seen something. I need to find out what."

Paul's eyes twinkled as he gazed at her. "I feel sorry for the perpetrator." He reached across the table and took her hand. "He doesn't have a chance with you on his trail."

Chapter Four

Kate woke earlier than usual Friday morning, and her first coherent thoughts were about Skip. Had he returned home? Was he all right?

She slipped on a robe and slippers and padded into the kitchen. Pushing back her sleep-tossed hair, she retrieved the coffee grinder and beans from the cupboard.

And when he did return home, how would Skip mollify his disgruntled boss? Kate pulverized the coffee beans and inhaled deeply as the rich aroma of fresh coffee filled the air.

With automatic movements, she put a filter and water in the coffeemaker, added the grounds, and turned on the machine. The gurgling and sighing it made were comforting to Kate as she sat down at the scarred oak table to wait for the coffee.

"Lord, I don't know what's up with that boy, but keep him safe. He's a nice young man. I didn't mean to make things worse for him with the sheriff. If he's chasing an escaped prisoner, Lord, keep them both safe."

The coffeemaker beeped. Kate sighed. "Amen." She walked over to the kitchen counter and reached for a mug.

"Would you mind making that two mugs?" a deep voice said behind her, nearly making her jump.

She looked over her shoulder. "Paul. I didn't hear you come in." She took a second mug from the cupboard.

"I know." He came up behind her and massaged her shoulders. "You were praying. I didn't want to interrupt you."

She handed him a fresh mug of coffee.

"Do you have a plan for today?" Paul asked as they moved into the living room.

Kate sat in her favorite chair in front of the fireplace and looked up at him. "I'm going to check at Town Hall and see if Skip's back. If he's not, I may go by his apartment or pay a visit to his mother. Someone must know where he's gone. First, though, I need to read my Bible and ask the Lord for direction."

"May I join you today?"

"Oh yes. I've been reading in Psalms."

Paul got his well-worn leather Bible, then sat across from her and opened it near the middle. "Here's a good one for today. I'll read to you."

Kate leaned back and closed her eyes.

"Psalm forty-six. 'God is our refuge and strength, an ever-present help in trouble. Therefore we will not fear, though the earth give way and the mountains fall into the heart of the sea, though its waters roar and foam and the mountains quake with their surging. Selah.'"

Paul's rich voice washed over Kate like a soothing balm. He spoke the beautiful promises with such quiet conviction, her heart filled with a song of praise as she listened.

When Kate opened her eyes, her precious husband was still, his head bent and his eyes closed, talking to the Lord whom he loved and served with all his heart. She closed her eyes and joined him, silently, in prayer. Somehow, the Lord would be with Skip and would show her a way to make amends.

THE SUN SHINING THROUGH the wisps of chimney smoke gave a yellowed hue to the ribbons of gray hanging over the town. Kate loved the smell of burning wood, especially the cedar and the apple wood Paul had gotten from a parishioner who had cleared an old orchard.

She'd planned to stop at the Mercantile for chocolate chips and then go by Skip's apartment, but a sheriff's department SUV was parked in front of Town Hall when she drove by.

Relieved, she parked next to it and hurried past the bare trees lining the walk and up the concrete steps, thinking about how she would apologize for her part in rousing Sheriff Roberts' ire.

A deputy stood just inside the doorway. She didn't recognize him. An older man, about her own age, she guessed. Portly. She could see past him. The area in front of the display case was cordoned off with crime-scene tape.

"Do you have business here, ma'am?" he asked.

"I came to see Deputy Spencer," she said.

"He isn't here. Your name?"

"Kate Hanlon." She looked at his name badge. "Deputy Martin, I'm the one who discovered that the commemorative coin is missing."

"In that case, the sheriff will want to take a statement. Please come into the office. I'll call him."

As they entered the office, Kate said, "Have you been with the department long?"

"I'm part of the sheriff's reserve. I'm retired highway patrol, but I fill in as a deputy when they need help. Skip asked me to cover for him. Have a seat Ms. Hanlon." Deputy Martin indicated a chair, then he picked up the phone and punched in a series of numbers.

"You've spoken to Skip Spencer?" Kate hesitated.

The deputy shook his head. "I didn't talk to him, but he left me a message yesterday. Said he had an emergency and had to go out of town. Didn't say where or how long he'd be gone. I didn't hear the message until late last night. Sheriff believes he was covering his tracks."

"Do you think he could be out looking for the prisoner? Maybe he escaped and stole the coin." Kate lowered herself into the chair.

Deputy Martin shook his head. "If so, Skip should have reported it to the sheriff, and he'd have taken his squad car. Makes no sense. He left the keys hanging behind the door. I went and picked it up at his apartment."

"Have you talked to everyone who visited Town Hall yesterday? Maybe someone saw something."

"Not yet," the deputy said. "Rest assured, we will fully investigate." He held the receiver up to his ear. "Sheriff, I have a woman here, Ms. Hanlon, who claims she's the one who discovered the coin theft here at Town Hall yesterday. Do you want me to take a statement?"

Deputy Martin listened for a moment, then held out the phone for Kate. "He wants to talk to you."

"Oh. Thank you." Kate got up and took the phone. "Hello, Sheriff."

"You amaze me, Kate. How do you always manage to become involved in every incident in Copper Mill?"

"I, ah . . ."

"Never mind. You must have noticed the coin was missing right after we spoke, right?"

"Exactly." She recounted the story to the sheriff. "Evidently, the coin was stolen."

"Allegedly. Have you seen or spoken to Deputy Spencer?"

"No, I was hoping he'd be back this morning. This isn't like him. I'm afraid something may have happened to him."

"I assume you realize he's a primary person of interest in this case."

She heard the sheriff sigh.

"Anything you learn pertaining to his whereabouts and actions will be appreciated," he added.

"Of course." Kate was startled. The sheriff didn't usually like her meddling in police business. He must have been more concerned than he let on.

"Will you let me know if you hear from him, for my peace of mind?" she asked.

"All right. Good-bye, Kate. Let me talk to my deputy again."

Chapter Five

Someone must have seen something, Kate thought as she walked down the hall to the mayor's office.

Clara glanced up over the top of her glasses when she entered. "Good morning, Kate. May I help you?"

"I hope so. I saw a tall, thin man leaving the building yesterday when I came in, and I'm trying to find out more about him. He had on a green wool jacket. Did he come in here by any chance?"

"Sure did," Clara said, nodding. "He was part of a group. They were here Wednesday for a tour and came back for local information. They expected to find tours of the mines. I gave them a chamber of commerce brochure on the area."

Clara tsk-tsked. "Why they'd want to go poking around those old mines and tromping around the countryside in this weather is beyond me." She shook her head. "They're from up north, you know. I suppose they expected us to be warm."

"From what I understand, this cold is unusual, even for Copper Mill," Kate said, tapping her fingers on the counter. "You mentioned that Gertie Crowe cleaned on Tuesday," she said in what she hoped was a nonchalant manner. "What other days does she come in? Has she been here since Tuesday?"

"She was here early this morning. She cleans before Town Hall opens on Fridays and in the afternoon on Tuesdays." She narrowed her eyes at Kate. "She avoids me since I told her she needed to clean the baseboards."

"Well, you can never be too clean, can you?" Kate knew that gaining Clara's trust was going to be important in getting more help from the woman. "You have such a good memory, I'm wondering if you can help me with one more thing. Do you remember the last time you saw the coin?"

The corners of Clara's mouth turned up just a bit. "I looked at it Wednesday at noon." She smoothed down the hem of her blouse. "I remember because I saw a copper plate backed by royal blue in a catalog and thought it would look nice with our coin." She pursed her lips. "We must get it back," she added emphatically.

"Have you thought of anyone who might have taken the coin?" Kate noted the hint of desperation in Clara's voice.

"Not a soul, other than Skip Spencer, of course. I hate to think one of my former students would stoop to breaking the law." Clara got a far-off look in her eyes, as if she were looking at something in the distance. "I tried to instill good values in my charges, but a teacher can only do so much."

"I'm sure you taught your students well," Kate said, and Clara smiled.

Kate wondered if the sheriff knew about the visitors at the hotel. The sheriff, the deputy, and Clara were all using deductive reasoning and coming up with Skip as the most likely suspect. But with Skip, you couldn't always apply logic.

Kate thanked Clara for her help and turned to go. As she left the mayor's office, she saw Lucy Mae Briddle go into the multipurpose room down the hall and decided to follow her.

"Lucy Mae," Kate called, hurrying after her. "How are you?"

The mayor's wife turned to see who was calling her. "Oh, hello, Kate. I'm glad to see you here. I assume you're on the trail of our coin thief. I told Lawton you would get our coin back if anyone could."

"I'd sure like to." Kate stepped inside the room. "Clara tells me you're the one to thank for the excellent condition of Town Hall. She said you keep an eye on many of the details around here."

"Indeed I do. You have no idea the demands of Lawton's job as Copper Mill's mayor. He simply cannot worry about Town Hall details. I tried to help in the office for a while, but I have so many other duties, just keeping up with his social calendar, you know." Lucy Mae patted her tightly permed hair at her temple. "I help him where I can."

"I know you put in a lot of time here. You're around so much, surely you see lots of things others don't." Kate watched Lucy Mae, waiting. "Do you remember the last time you saw the coin by any chance?"

"Of course. It was in the case when I left at four o'clock Wednesday afternoon. I know, because I checked for fingerprints. Gertie cleaned the glass on Tuesday." She gave her head a short nod. Her curls didn't budge.

"Did you happen to see the people who are staying at the hotel? I saw a tall man leaving Town Hall Thursday afternoon."

"Oh yes. Lawton told me he gave them a tour. They're here from Connecticut. Snowbirds, I believe. They viewed the case Wednesday morning. They didn't leave so much as a finger-print on the glass." She tsk-tsked. "Can't say the same for the floor, though. Those men and their heavy boots."

"We don't get that many snowbirds around here, do we?"

"Not usually. This group told Lawton they're very inter-ested in our heritage." She frowned. "You don't think they stole the coin, do you? They seemed like nice people when I greeted them."

"Our history draws a lot of tourists. It's probably coinci-dence." But they had taken a tour, Kate mused. Their visit narrowed the time line and added to Kate's list of suspects. "Did you come in Thursday?"

"No. I wish I had. I might have prevented the theft. Thursday I went to the beauty shop."

Kate wished she had been here too. As she left the build-ing, she thought about the reactions to the missing coin. She knew that coin was highly valued. In the years following the demise of mining in these parts, the coin reminded people of better times and symbolized hope that someday prosperity would return. Both Lucy Mae and Clara seemed more con-cerned about the coin than about Skip. Kate was interested in finding out what really happened to Skip, but she suspected that finding the coin might accomplish both goals.

THE SHERIFF'S SUSPICIONS about Skip's odd behavior and dis-appearance occupied Kate's thoughts as she left Town Hall and drove to Jim Hepburn's place. She'd met Jim a few times, though Paul knew him better from his work as a volunteer dogcatcher for the Copper Mill Humane Society. Skip rented an apartment over Jim's garage.

Kate guessed Skip hadn't returned when she saw that the old blue truck she'd seen him driving was missing. Jim's rusty old white pickup truck was parked in front of the house, so Kate got out of her car and went to see if Jim knew where Skip might have gone. She knocked on his front door. After a couple of minutes, Jim came to the door.

"Missus Hanlon, this is a surprise." He blinked and scratched his day-old stubble. "Would you like to come in?"

"No, thank you. I don't want to bother you. I'm just looking for Skip. Do you know where he might be?"

Jim ran his fingers through his unkempt hair. He frowned, drawing attention to the deep lines on his face and forehead. "Haven't seen him since he got into his truck and roared out of here yesterday morning."

"Is it a blue truck? I saw him leaving town in it."

"Yup. He bought it awhile back to fix up." Jim scratched his head and frowned. "I helped him rebuild the engine, but it ain't exactly road-ready yet."

"Did you talk to him at all? Did he say where he was going?"

Jim shook his head. "Just said he had to leave for a while. Some kind of emergency. He threw a duffle bag in the back of his truck—same bag he takes his laundry in to his mom's place every week. Asked me to collect his mail 'cause he didn't have time to stop by the post office."

Jim shrugged. "It's none of my business, but that boy tends to get scatterbrained, if you know what I mean. He usually tells me if he's going to be gone. Sheriff came by last night looking for him. He was in a foul mood. Said he'd send someone for the SUV, then Hugh Martin came and got it."

"Would he have taken his laundry to his mother's?" Kate asked.

"Don't know, but that's what I told the sheriff. Skip's a good renter. Never causes trouble. Visits his mother regular-like. We work on our trucks together, so I've got to know him real good. He doesn't drink or smoke or swear. Good kid."

"I know. That's why I'm concerned about him," Kate said. "I noticed his truck is pretty old. What model is it? Is it considered a classic?"

"Well, now, it's old enough to be a classic, but it's not exactly a fine specimen. It's a 1969 Ford F-100 Ranger pickup. A good truck in its day. Needs more work than it's worth, in my opinion. Skip's bound and determined to fix 'er up, though."

Jim rubbed the scruff on his chin. "I heard about that coin going missing. Sheriff didn't say, but news travels, you know. I figured he'd want to search the apartment, but he didn't ask. Kind of surprised me."

"The sheriff follows procedure. He won't look until he has a search warrant."

"Sure enough. I bet you're right. And I'll have to let him in."

"Do you think Skip took the coin?" Kate asked, studying Jim's face.

"No way. That boy doesn't have a dishonest bone in his body."

"I expect the sheriff has talked to his mother. She's probably beside herself with worry," Kate said.

She looked up at the windows of Skip's apartment.

Getting a look inside might give some clues about where he'd gone and what had precipitated his rush out of town. But would that violate his privacy? Normally she wouldn't consider probing into his private life.

Kate thought about her own motives. Skip had the right to go where he desired and even make decisions that jeopardized his job, but he was suspected of robbery. That changed everything. She couldn't prove his innocence if she couldn't find him.

"I'd feel a lot better if I knew he's all right. If I could look in his apartment, I might be able to discover if he needs help."

Jim's brow wrinkled as if he were battling the same indecision. "If Skip's in trouble, I want to help too. I've got the key. Nothing says we can't look. After all, I'm his landlord."

Jim got his keys and unlocked the door. The apartment was dark and cold. He flipped on a light, revealing clutter, but Kate wasn't sure if it was because Skip left in a hurry or if it was his typical bachelor existence.

Jim headed to the kitchen, and Kate spotted an envelope in the trashcan that had scribbling on it. She picked it up gingerly, holding it by the corners. A Web site address and what looked like names of vehicle parts were written on the back of it. Beneath it was a grayed imprint, almost like a faint carbon copy.

Kate held the envelope up to a window. The impression looked like a name: Jamie, no, Jayme Johnson. She jotted down the name and the Web site URL, then dropped the envelope back into the trash. As she did, she noticed a crumpled paper with the logo of the Mid-Cumberland Bank and Trust.

She hated to be so nosy, but any clue might help. She took

the paper out and smoothed it. What the paper showed aston-
ished Kate. Skip had withdrawn a large sum of money from a
savings account, over three thousand dollars. According to the
receipt, his account now had a zero balance.

Why would Skip withdraw his entire savings? She put the
slip back in the trash. The sheriff would see it when he came
back to search. She had no doubt about the conclusions he'd
draw.

Kate wandered into the tiny kitchen. Pop cans, an empty
microwave popcorn bag, and an empty TV-dinner tray sat on
the counter. A frying pan was soaking in the sink.

She didn't find any other scrawled notes or addresses. An
outdated magnetic calendar from a pizza parlor in Pine Ridge
stuck to the refrigerator door.

"Not much in the refrigerator," Jim said, holding the door
open. He picked up a carton of milk and shook it. "Almost
empty. There's part of a carton of eggs, a couple slices of bacon,
and a couple doggy bags from the Country Diner."

"The cupboards don't have much more," Kate commented,
looking at the assortment of mismatched dishes and cans of
food. "Tuna, pork and beans, peanut butter, Sloppy Joe sauce,
and applesauce. He must eat out a lot."

"Yeah. He also goes to his mom's a lot. I've gone with him
a time or two. She's a good cook."

In the bedroom, they found a few articles of clothing on
the floor. Skip's uniform was hung neatly in the closet. Several
empty hangers indicated he'd taken clothes with him.

Obviously he'd left in a hurry, but Kate was relieved to see
signs that he intended to return, like the pan in the sink. Why
would he put it to soak unless he planned to come back and

wash it? He'd left some kind of charger plugged in. His video-game controller sat on a makeshift coffee table in front of a television. A card table in the corner held a computer and a half-empty soda can. None were large items. Surely if he intended to leave permanently, he'd have taken them along.

"I don't see anything that indicates where he went," Kate said.

"Me, neither." Jim followed Kate out and locked the door behind him. "I sure hope that boy isn't in some kind of trouble."

"Other than the facts that he left without telling anyone, and both a prisoner and a commemorative coin are missing, I'm sure he's fine," Kate said with a half smile. Jim didn't need to know that she'd found incriminating evidence, but she was filled with concern. How could she clear Skip's name with all this evidence mounting against him?

"Well, Skip speaks highly of you, Missus Hanlon. If anyone can help him, you can. Let me know if I can help. I get around town a lot. I know just about everyone."

"Thanks, Jim. Please call me if you hear from Skip."

Kate left Jim on his front porch, staring off toward town. She hoped he might remember some comment Skip made that would give them a clue, any clue that could help prove his innocence. Otherwise, Kate realized, she had nothing to go on.

IT WAS ELEVEN when Kate left Jim's. She tried to sort her thoughts about Skip as she drove to Skip's mother's house. Since moving to Copper Mill, she'd personally seen his dedication to serving the townspeople. He guarded Copper Mill with enthusiasm. She believed he truly wanted to uphold the law and help others.

His tendency to jump before looking where he'd land created many of his problems. He didn't think through his actions to see the consequences. Kate thought his impulsiveness exacerbated his klutziness. *If he'd only slow down . . .* To Kate's mind, he couldn't be guilty of anything more than poor judgment.

She barely knew Dolores Spencer, but Skip's attentiveness to his mother told of a good relationship, and that, to Kate, spoke volumes. Kate cherished her relationship with her own adult children.

Dolores lived in a modest one-story home. A perfectly trimmed boxwood hedge bordered the small front lawn, now browned from the onset of winter. Rose bushes were pruned and mulched against frosty nights, and leaves had been raked and removed from beneath the silver bell tree, with its little winged flowers still clinging to the bare branches. Kate wondered if Dolores did all the gardening or if Skip helped her.

When she rang the doorbell, a woman came to the door. She was average height, with dark, curly hair. She left the screen door shut. "Can I help you?"

"I'm Kate Hanlon. Is Dolores at home?" she asked.

"She's busy." The woman had one hand on the doorjamb and the other on the door, as if guarding the entrance.

"I'm a friend of her son, Skip . . ."

The woman raised her eyebrows. "Skip isn't here," she said.

"I know. If you could tell Dolores I'm here. I'd like to talk to her."

"Who is it, Trixie?" a voice called from the back of the house. Dolores came into view.

"Kate somebody," Trixie said.

Dolores came to the door and opened it wider. "Please

come in. Trixie, this is Kate Hanlon, wife of the minister at Faith Briar Church. Trixie used to live in Copper Mill," she explained. "She's visiting from Alabama."

Trixie stepped out of the way. From her cool reception, Kate surmised that the sheriff had already been there.

"Please, have a seat." Dolores sat on a recliner and draped a dishtowel over the arm of the chair. She was wearing jeans and an oversized T-shirt decorated with birdhouses.

Dolores looked tired. Kate knew that Skip's mother was a few years her senior, but she kept herself neat and trim. Her shoulder-length hair showed wisps of gray at the temples. She assumed Trixie was also in her late fifties. Trixie sat at one end of the couch; Kate sat at the other end.

"I hate to bother you, but I wondered if you'd heard from Skip," Kate said, diving right in. "I saw him yesterday as he was leaving town. He was driving an old truck, and it didn't look very reliable."

Dolores nodded. "I don't know why he bought that thing, but I wish he'd get rid of it. He thinks it's worth something. It's old enough, I suppose, but it's a junker, and I've told him so. The sheriff came by last night looking for Skip, and I told him the same thing I'm going to tell you." Dolores shook her head. "Skip didn't say anything to me about going out of town. I've tried calling him on his cell phone, but he hasn't returned my calls."

"He was on his way to Pine Ridge when I saw him," Kate said. "I stopped to tell him his rear tire looked loose. He didn't say where he was going, but he was in a hurry and seemed agitated about something. I hope he's all right."

"I'm sure he is, or I'd have heard, right? He goes fishing

once in a while, but not when he's supposed to be on duty, which is what's odd. Sheriff Roberts didn't say much, but he sure asked a lot of questions."

"Sounded like an interrogation to me," Trixie said. She sniffed disdainfully. "I told Dee she shouldn't answer without a lawyer present."

"I don't need a lawyer," Dolores said. "I haven't done anything wrong." She pursed her lips. "I can't blame the sheriff for being upset. He can't protect the citizens of the county if his deputies take off without giving notice. I just don't understand that boy. I tried to raise him with a strong work ethic and values. He got a good job, and what does he do? Goes off without telling his boss."

"Or his mother." Trixie shook her head.

"He could lose his job, behaving that way, and I can't blame the sheriff." She sighed.

"Now, Dee, you did your best, raising Skip by yourself. Being a single parent of a teenaged boy is hard. I know. I'm lucky my son turned out as well as he did. He has a very successful business and shares his house with me. I couldn't ask for a more attentive son. Even here, he calls me every day to let me know he's all right. Oh dear." Trixie looked stricken, like she just realized she'd said something wrong. "Your Skip is a nice, polite boy. 'Course, I haven't been around him for several years." She looked away, staring out the window.

Dolores gave Kate a helpless look. Kate didn't think Trixie's attempt at reassurance helped.

"Can you remember the last conversation you had with Skip?" Kate asked.

"Yes. He came for dinner Tuesday night. I fixed chicken-fried steak with tomato gravy, cornbread, and apple pie. I haven't made it in a long time. Trixie remembered it and asked me to make it. It's one of Skip's favorites too. It was one of those things that got us talking about old times. We were laughing over things the boys did when they were younger."

"Did Skip talk about somewhere he'd like to go?"

"No. Well, he mentioned a fishing tournament, but that's in the spring. He thought maybe Trixie's son Gary might want to join them. He knows some of the other guys from high school."

"I see. Dolores, I probably sound nosy, but please let me know if you think of *anything* else, no matter how insignificant it might seem. We've got to get to the bottom of this."

"I know you're trying to help. Skip trusts you, Kate. So do I. He told me you're real smart about figuring things out. I wish I knew what to do. He's never done anything like this before."

Dolores didn't seem to be aware of the missing coin, and Kate didn't want to distress her more, so she decided not to say anything about it. She rose.

"Could I have his cell phone number? I'll try reaching him too."

Dolores wrote down the number and gave it to Kate.

"Thank you. Paul and I will keep Skip in our prayers. When you hear from him, would you please let me know?"

Dolores walked with Kate to the door. "Yes. Thank you. I appreciate your concern and your prayers. That boy needs a guardian angel, I tell you."

Kate heard the door close behind her as she walked to her

car. She wondered why the sheriff hadn't asked about the coin when he'd come, then she decided he probably hadn't wanted to upset or antagonize Skip's mother in case Skip called home. Dolores was right. Her son needed a guardian angel. One with fortitude and lots of energy.

Chapter Six

While Kate stirred cookie batter after lunch, she studied the list of visitors she'd noted from her conversation with Clara. Something about the automatic motions of measuring, whipping, stirring, and spooning dollops of dough on cookie sheets helped her organize her thoughts.

Kate had called and left a message on Skip's cell phone. Like Dolores, all she could do was wait for him to return her call. In the meantime, she turned to the facts she'd determined so far.

According to her list, Fred Cowan, who owned the pharmacy, had been to Town Hall. Then there were the visitors staying at the Hamilton Springs Hotel. As tourists, they might have seen something without recognizing it wasn't normal. Kate wondered if one of them took the coin.

She slid a pan of cookies into the oven, set the timer, then started filling another cookie sheet. She glanced at the list again. Lucy Mae's verification of the timing eliminated a lot of people. Arlene Jacobs' class met on Wednesday morning, so it ruled them out, because the coin had been there after that. On Thursday, no one had used the multipurpose room.

Skip lived a quiet life, according to his landlord, and he was kind and helpful to his mother. Skip had confided to Kate that he wanted to prove himself to the sheriff and advance to sergeant someday. Leaving without notice could ruin his chances. Being indicted for stealing a coin certainly would. It didn't make sense.

The oven timer went off as Paul entered the kitchen. He'd been working in his office for the afternoon. Kate put on oven mitts and retrieved the cookie sheet, sliding another in its place.

"*Mmm*. Smells good in here." He helped himself to a warm cookie. "Working on a puzzle?"

"Why, of course," Kate said in her sweetest Southern accent. She transferred the cookies from the pan to a sheet of parchment paper. "I have to tell you, honey, I'm completely buffaloed about Skip. I've talked with the deputy replacing Skip, the sheriff, his mother, and his landlord. He's disappeared off the face of the earth."

"And do you think he took the coin before he left?"

"The circumstantial evidence says yes. But I don't think so. I can't prove it yet, but my intuition, my instincts, and everything I know about Skip tell me no. I feel certain he did not steal that coin. The only alternative I can come up with is that he's chasing an escaped prisoner who did take it. But the new deputy didn't see that as a viable option. Says Skip would have called the sheriff to report it."

"But why wouldn't he have taken his police SUV?"

"I don't know." Kate shrugged. "Maybe it was out of gas."

"Didn't you tell me he came out of the Quik Stop when he cut you off?"

"Good point. He must have stopped for gas. Another reason my theory is off. Maybe his errand is personal."

"Sounds like it to me," Paul said, reaching for another cookie.

"Good thing I made a double batch of cookies, just in case you want to go calling," Kate said, chuckling. "I thought you might want to meet Sheena's husband, Tom."

Paul gave her a knowing smile. "You guessed correctly. I got their address. Give me a few minutes, and I'll be on my way while those cookies are still warm." He poured a cup of coffee, picked up one more cookie, and escaped to his study.

PAUL PARKED IN FRONT OF A SMALL, rundown house on the outskirts of Copper Mill. He double-checked the address he'd gotten off a notice posted on the bulletin board at the Mercantile.

Skeletons of tall, winter-killed weeds surrounded the house that had little yard. The blotchy turquoise exterior of the house needed painting, and the roof tiles were falling off. A broken window had been sealed off with cardboard on the inside.

Paul suspected the house had sat empty for some time before Sheena and Tom moved in. He picked up the plate of cookies Kate sent along and went up the walk to the front door.

Loud rock music and the sound of hammering came from inside. Paul knocked on the door several times. He was about to leave when there was a break in the music. He knocked again. He heard something loud, like something dropped, then the door opened.

A tall, thin young man wearing a dusty black baseball cap peered out at him through a torn screen door.

"Hi, I'm Paul Hanlon. Are you Tom?"

"Yeah. You must be the guy who gave Sheena your card. I was going to call you."

"That's all right. I saw your ad on the board at the Mercantile. Sheena told me you're a carpenter. I thought I'd stop by and see if I can help introduce you to some of the townspeople, and maybe we can find some work for you."

"That's mighty kind of you, Mr. Hanlon. I'd be obliged to find some work. Not many openings around here."

"I suppose winter's a slow time for construction," Paul said. "Oh, I brought you some cookies. My wife thought you might like them."

Tom smiled and opened the door. "Thanks," he said, reaching for the plate. "Come on in. The place is a mess. I promised the landlord I'd do some fix-up work in exchange for rent."

Paul entered the nearly bare room. A pair of matching green recliners looked new. A square of unfinished wood on cinder blocks supported a large flat-screen television set against one wall. A small coffee table made from cinder blocks and plywood sat in the middle of the room. There didn't seem to be any other furniture in the house. A door led to a small bedroom. He could see a mattress on the floor.

"Would you like a cup of coffee?" Tom offered. "It's strong, and I don't have any cream, but I have sugar."

"No thanks. I've had my quota for the day," Paul said.

He followed Tom into the tiny kitchen at the back. A chipped, stained sink, a two-burner stove and ancient refrigerator with a rounded top took up most of the room. Empty Styrofoam containers and soda cans were piled in one corner. A state-of-the-art, self-grinding, stainless-steel coffeepot sat on a makeshift plywood counter that had rough edges and was only partially nailed down.

"The kitchen's a mess. The counter looked like someone chopped it up for firewood," Tom explained. "I got this from the dump." He pointed to the corner. "I found those cabinets too. Not fancy, but it'll be better than nothing."

"Looks like you're resourceful," Paul said. "What kind of carpentry do you do?"

"You name it. I've done everything from framing to finish work. I worked for a construction company in Birmingham, building houses, and I've done a lot of remodel work for people."

"Why did you leave Birmingham?" Paul asked as Tom gestured toward one of the recliners in the living room. "I would think jobs would be more plentiful there."

Paul took a seat, and Tom sat down in the other chair.

"Not so good as you'd think," he said. "Besides, Sheena wants kids, and I don't want to raise a family in the city. Rent's cheaper here too. I plan to start my own business, but I need to get some jobs. It takes money to get started."

"Do you have your own tools?"

"I have some from my dad. He was a finish carpenter. Really good too. He taught me. He gave me some of his tools to help me get started."

"That should make getting jobs easier. I'm planning a small

project putting a workbench and shelves in my garage. I'm not much of a handyman, so I'd be interested in getting your ideas."

"Sure. I'd be glad to take a look."

"Good. Does Sheena work every night? We'd love to have the two of you come for dinner some night, and afterward I can show you the garage."

"That would be great. She just works part-time, but she's off Tuesdays for sure."

"Tuesday would be good, say five thirty? Let me give you directions."

"We have your card. We'll find it." Tom walked to the door with Paul. He shook Paul's hand, then shoved his hands in his back pockets as he said good-bye.

"I'll see you Tuesday then," Paul said as he went out the door.

"Sounds good."

Paul was pleased. He'd gotten past the front door, and Tom had accepted his invitation. Paul looked forward to having someone with some experience take a look at his garage plans. He'd looked at layouts in project periodicals, but he wanted the job to be simple. A workbench and some kind of cabinets or shelving, that's all. Kate knew exactly how she wanted things arranged in the house, but he wanted the garage to be his own personal project.

SATURDAY MORNING, Kate went through her usual routine, rising early, slipping on her favorite soft robe and slippers, shuffling to the kitchen with sleepy steps, grinding coffee beans, then inhaling the fresh, delightful aroma that swept away the last vestiges of sleep as she made coffee.

Glancing out the window, she shivered. A glaze of frost covered the backyard. The outdoor thermometer registered twenty-eight degrees. She started a fire in the fireplace, then settled in her favorite chair in the living room with a mug of coffee and her Bible to have her devotions.

Skip was uppermost in her mind, so she went to the Lord, praying for Skip's safety and for the circumstances around him to sort themselves out and reveal his innocence. She prayed for Dolores. Sooner or later she would hear about the stolen coin and the sheriff's suspicions about Skip. Then she prayed for Sheena and Tom.

Although she hadn't met the young man and barely knew the girl, she understood the difficulties of settling into a new town. At least Paul had employment and they became part of a built-in church family when they moved to Copper Mill. Sheena and Tom didn't have it so easy.

Paul went through the living room on his way to the kitchen. She heard him pour himself a mug of coffee just as the doorbell rang. Kate finished her prayer and said "Amen" as the bell rang again. She fled to her room and quickly donned her blue sweat suit and ran a brush through her hair.

Sheriff Roberts was standing with Paul in the living room when she came out. The sheriff removed his hat and apologized for intruding so early.

"Not a problem. Would you like a cup of coffee?" Paul asked.

"No. Thanks." Sheriff Roberts held his hat in his hand and fingered it nervously

"Please have a seat," Kate offered, sitting on one of the armchairs.

"Thanks." He sat down on the couch across from her, and Paul took the other chair.

The sheriff looked from Kate to Paul, then back to Kate. His jaw tightened visibly before he spoke, then he let out a sigh, as if resigned.

"Kate, I went to Skip's apartment this morning with a search warrant. Jim told me he took you up to the apartment, and you both spent time looking around. I wish you hadn't done that. Did you touch or remove anything from the apartment?"

His question surprised Kate, but then she reminded herself that he had to investigate everything and everyone possible. She swallowed her impulse to jump to her own defense and looked him straight in the eye. "I didn't remove or move anything. I was looking for some way to help figure out where he is. I know Clara implicated Skip, but there are lots of other people who could have taken the coin, and I'm worried about him."

"We'll look into every possibility."

Kate knew the sheriff was a fair man, but even she had to admit that the case against Skip seemed to be growing. She hated to mention the savings-withdrawal slip, but she couldn't shield Skip either. "I did notice a receipt in the trash. Skip took money out of his savings before he left. There were also notes about truck parts and a Web site."

"I saw those items. It appears he removed all his assets. Skip left in a panic. Your statements verify that fact. You told me Skip was in a hurry, driving a truck that wasn't reliable, that he was agitated and secretive."

"Not secretive exactly. He was a man on a mission. I didn't

know about his escaped prisoner at the time. Perhaps he was chasing the man. Maybe the escapee stole the town's commemorative coin?"

"I've thought of that too, but there's no evidence of an escape. By all appearances, Skip unlocked the door and let him out. He may be an accomplice, or maybe Skip let him out so he wouldn't have a witness."

"Who was this prisoner? Have you looked for him?"

"He's a local man, picked up for unpaid tickets, driving with expired plates, and driving without a license. Just misdemeanors. No history of criminal charges, but he couldn't make bail, so he was awaiting a hearing. He's not dangerous."

Sheriff Roberts ran his hand across the smooth tan fabric of the couch. "We checked out his house, but there's no one at home. A neighbor saw him come and get his wife, and they put a suitcase in the car and drove off in a hurry. We've got an APB out for them. The jail keys were hanging right there. Someone—most likely Skip—used the key, then replaced it. I don't see why an escaped prisoner would take the time to put the key back, let alone bury it under a pile of keys."

Kate couldn't refute his logic. She looked down at her slippers, not really seeing them, thinking over the sheriff's comments and what she knew so far.

"I spoke to Lucy Mae Briddle," she said finally. "She positively saw the coin in place late Wednesday afternoon, so it was taken sometime between Wednesday afternoon and Thursday afternoon. Anyone could have come in, gotten the key, and made the substitution." She shrugged. "What about fingerprints on the token and the glass?"

"We've dusted for prints, and we're waiting for a read on

those. I won't leave any stone unturned. I just hope we come up with some evidence soon, otherwise Skip has a lot to answer for."

"Did you tell Skip's mother that you suspect him of stealing the coin?" Kate asked.

"No. He's still just a person of interest in the case. I've talked to her, and she doesn't seem to know where he's gone. No sense making her more upset if I can help it."

Kate could see it pained Sheriff Roberts to accuse his deputy. "That's kind of you. I know Skip makes rash decisions at times," she said gently, "but he loves enforcing the law and protecting the people and property of Copper Mill. I'm certain he did not take that coin."

The sheriff sighed. "I appreciate your loyalty, Kate, andyou're right. But for now, I have to go with facts. I have to find him and bring him in for questioning."

Chapter Seven

L ater that morning, after Kate finished her housecleaning, she made a trip to the library. Her best friend Livvy was seated in the children's section, leaning forward, waving her arms as she read a story to a rapt group of children.

Kate went upstairs to begin her search. She wasn't exactly sure how to begin, so she went first to the section on local history. The books on the shelves were leaning over where many other books had been removed. All of the books on Copper Mill, Harrington County, or the mines were gone. She looked around at the tables. A woman with two elementary-aged children had a couple of books open, but not enough to account for the empty shelves.

Kate opened her handbag and dug out the note where she'd copied a name and Web site URL off the envelope in Skip's trash. She went to a computer and logged on, trying the Web site first, typing it into the address bar. A site for vehicle parts came up.

Kate thought of the vehicle Skip was driving: a Ford pickup, almost forty years old. She clicked on Ford trucks.

A page of pictures came up. There it was, a 1969 Ford Ranger, refurbished. Even though it appeared to be in much better condition than Skip's truck, it looked similar to the pickup she'd followed to Pine Ridge. Even restored, the truck wasn't valuable.

Kate surfed around the Web site. If he'd ordered parts, she doubted they'd arrived before he took off; otherwise the truck wouldn't have been in such bad condition.

Kate clicked on several links, trying to find a clue to Skip's whereabouts. After several fruitless rabbit trails, she clicked on a page about installation instructions. At the bottom of the page, she found a link called "How Stuff Works." Clicking on it, she came upon instruction manuals for various models, a link to expert help, and a forum.

She clicked on the forum. She had seen these kinds of discussion boards before, and once she had found her way to the site, it allowed her to look at recent posts. She went back as far as the previous week. Nothing. It wouldn't allow her to go further without registering, but she could register free.

Kate hated to sign up for things that would fill her in-box with junk mail, but she needed to trace Skip. It asked for a user name. She thought for a moment. Her children were PKs, for preacher's kids. She typed in "PWKatie," for preacher's wife. That ought to work. It went right through.

She picked a simple password, and she was in. Pleased, she scrolled back a week, then another, scanning the various posts.

A post jumped out at her. Jjohns wanted to know how to fix a window that stuck. Kate guessed Jjohns could be short for Jayme Johnson, the name on the same envelope Kate had fished out of the garbage can.

Several posts later, Coppercop answered Jjohns. Kate laughed out loud. Not only was Skip a cop from Copper Mill, his hair was a bright reddish copper color. Unmistakable. It *had* to be Skip.

Excited, Kate read his answer about taking the door panel off and regluing the window to the bottom track. Several posts later, Jjohns asked another question of Coppercop, and two exchanges later, Coppercop suggested they take the conversation offline so he could answer all Jjohn's questions. Coppercop gave his e-mail address. Kate wrote it down.

She left a question for Jjohns, asking if the window had gotten fixed and to please contact her. Kate took a chance and gave her e-mail address. She wrote down the Internet address for the forum, then logged out and opened her e-mail. She composed an e-mail to Coppercop's address.

Dear Skip. Call me. It's urgent.

She signed it Kate and gave her e-mail address, home phone, and cell phone number, then hit Send.

That her search yielded *anything* about Skip exhilarated Kate. He hadn't returned her message to his cell phone, but perhaps he would check his e-mail and answer her.

Still excited, she ran a search of Copper Mill's history. It brought up a photocopy of the newspaper article about the coin and the mine celebration. Kate had read the same article in the Town Hall showcase, but she read it again, jotting down notes.

The Copper Mill coin was gold overlaid with copper, which would increase its value. The coin was a little smaller than a silver dollar, so Kate guessed it weighed approximately an ounce. Even at that, she couldn't imagine the coin being worth thousands of dollars. She found a coin dealer and sent an e-mail, describing the coin, the size, and the date and Superior Mint and Casting Company where it was made, hoping she could discover the coin's value.

Then she began a new search, typing "commemorative" into the search window. Before she could add "coin," a larger window popped open and a list of previous similar word searches came up. She stared at the selections. Several included the word *copper*. That seemed odd to her. She deleted her entry and tried again. She typed in "copper." The window popped open and listed entries for *copper coins*, *copper mining*, *copper mills*, *commemorative copper coins*.

Kate thought of a lot of words that went with copper. Pipes. Kettles. Pans. Wire. Why didn't any of them come up? She clicked on the link to commemorative copper coins. That brought up links to manufacturers and suppliers, the United States Mint, coins with animals, foreign coins, and railroad coins. There were thousands of links to coins.

She clicked on several coin vendors and coin guides, looking for the Copper Mill coin, but found nothing remotely similar.

Kate quit that search and tried "copper mining." One of the links led to the history of the Copper Basin area. A site about the Old Copper Road didn't mention a coin or commemorative medallion or anything close. The links from previous searches all led to dead ends, but the fact that someone had looked seemed significant. The information someone sought was too similar to the missing coin to be coincidence.

She was reasonably certain they hadn't found the Copper Mill coin.

Kate logged off and went downstairs to ask about the missing historical books. Livvy was talking to a patron. Kate moved to the side to wait without being intrusive. She glanced over at a rolling cart the librarians used to transport books. The cart was filled with history books.

She sidled closer and read the titles. *Mining in the Copper Basin. History of Harrington County. Copper Veins. On the Old Copper Road. Bonanza*, she thought. She'd discovered the missing books. Too bad locating the coin wasn't as simple.

"Find what you needed?" Livvy asked, coming over to her.

"Not exactly. Looks like someone was here before me, though."

Livvy glanced at the cart. Her eyebrows rose. "The cart was empty when I started the story hour. I'll see what I can find out when Morty gets back from his lunch break."

"Thanks. I'll come back next week and look through the books." *Whoever else wants information on the Copper Mill commemorative coin may well be the thief*, Kate thought.

Chapter Eight

After lunch, Kate spent time in her studio. She had traced the lines of a flower petal on a sheet of variegated lavender and white wispy glass. As she poised her cutter to make a smooth, clean incision in the glass, the telephone rang. Paul had gone to the church office, so she was alone. She set the cutter down and answered the cordless phone.

"Hello, Kate speaking," she said.

"Kate, this is Abby Pippins. I have a prayer request to pass along for the prayer chain. It's for Wendy Hart—used to be Archer. I don't suppose you've met her. She attended Faith Briar as a teenager. Far as I know, she doesn't attend anywhere since she married Billy and her folks moved to Arizona.

"Anyways, one of the gals in my ceramics class told me Wendy is going through a difficult pregnancy, and she has to stay in the Pine Ridge Hospital until she delivers. She's diabetic, and they're worried about her blood sugar and toxemia."

"Oh dear. Poor thing." Kate jotted the name on a notepad. "I'll stop by to visit her when I go in with Paul. Maybe I can take something to cheer her up."

"I'm sure she'd appreciate a visit. She's a sweet young woman, and I don't think her life is very easy. She works at a day-care center in Pine Ridge, and now she's out of work. Her husband can't seem to hold down a job."

After Kate took down all of Wendy's information, she hung up the phone and sat for a moment to pray for her. She imagined how she'd feel if her own daughter was ill and her husband out of work. Kate's daughter Melissa lived in Atlanta, so Kate could get there in a matter of hours, but still, the thought made her heartsick for Wendy.

Kate wiped away a dab of moisture from the corner of her eye. Thoughts of her children often brought out her tender side, and she sympathized with other young people who were struggling to make their way in the world. Life seemed harder these days than when she was a young bride and mother. Perhaps the years had altered her memories, softening the hard times and accentuating the good times.

Still thinking about the pregnant Wendy, Kate got a drink of water. Maybe she could make a night-light for the baby's room, but that would have to wait until she finished her current projects. She'd seen some soft stuffed animals at the Mercantile. She'd take one to Wendy the next time Paul took his turn as chaplain at the Pine Ridge Hospital. Girls never outgrew a cuddly teddy bear or a lamb, no matter what their age. Later, Wendy could give it to the baby.

Kate thought about Skip's mother. She might need some comforting too. The sheriff's restraint in not telling Dolores that her son was a suspect in the coin theft gave Kate hope that he was considering other possibilities. Still, she knew Dolores would be worried about her son. Kate decided a visit was in order, so she arranged some cookies on a colorful paper plate and covered it with plastic wrap.

Within minutes, she'd parked her Honda and was walking up the sidewalk to Dolores Spencer's house. When she rang the doorbell, she caught a movement of the closed drapes in the front window. She glanced over in time to see a face disappear and the curtain fall back into place. The door opened a moment later.

"Come in," Dolores said. She made a quick motion, and her voice betrayed anxiety.

Kate stepped into the house, and Dolores locked the door.

"I hope this isn't a bad time," Kate said. "I've been thinking about you. I brought you some cookies." Kate could tell by her reddened eyes that Dolores had been crying.

"Thank you. Please come sit down." Dolores didn't take the plate but led her into the living room.

Kate set the plate on the coffee table. She removed her coat and sat on the couch. Dolores sat next to her and turned to face her, wringing her hands together in a show of agitation.

"I'm so glad you came, Kate. I don't know who to talk to." Her voice rose to a squeak.

"Where's Trixie? Did she leave?"

"No. She went to the store for me. I just can't face people right now." She cleared her throat. "Have you heard that the sheriff is asking everyone in town about Skip? I heard he thinks Skip might have taken that coin."

Kate nodded. There went her hope that Sheriff Roberts was considering other suspects. "I'm so sorry, Dolores."

"He kept asking me to think of places Skip might be. Here, I thought he was just concerned. But I don't know *anything*.

Besides, what kind of a mother does he think I am?" Dolores
said, raising her hands to her heart. "I've heard the rumors.
Everyone in town knows that the copper coin is missing and
that the sheriff blames Skip. I'm afraid people think I'm hiding
Skip or the coin or something."

They heard commotion at the front door. A key turned in
the lock, and Trixie kicked open the door with her foot, then
shouldered her way in, carrying two full grocery sacks and her
handbag, which was as large as the grocery sacks. "Oh, hello,"
she said.

Kate jumped up. "Let me help you."

"Thanks. If you don't mind, I'd appreciate the help. You
can bring in the other sacks of groceries. They're in Dee's car.
I left the door open."

Kate went out to retrieve the sacks. She shut the car door
and carried the groceries into the kitchen. One of the bags
held the unmistakable mouthwatering smell of fresh oranges,
but above that she caught a light sweet scent. It wasn't food.
Not perfume either, she thought. Something lighter. Perhaps
a laundry product or liquid hand soap.

Trixie was putting food in the refrigerator. "Just put them
on the counter," she said. "I'll take care of them later."

Trixie followed Kate into the living room and sat on the
couch next to Kate. She spied the cookies and helped herself
to one.

Kate turned to Dolores. "I want you to know I'm going to
do everything I can to prove Skip's innocence. Is there anything he might have said that could give us a clue to where he
went?"

Dolores frowned. "I've thought and thought. That fishing tournament with some of his friends isn't until spring. My brother-in-law lives in Ohio, and Skip has two cousins going to college there. That's all I know of."

"Have you spoken to your brother-in-law?" Kate asked.

"No. We haven't heard from him in years. He came to my husband's funeral, which surprised me. They weren't close. Then he disappeared from our lives. We got notices from the twins when they graduated from high school, and we sent money. Didn't even get a thank-you."

"Hmmph," Trixie snorted. "Young people today have no manners. At least your Skip and my Gary act like gentlemen. Skip called me ma'am and Mrs. Davenport. When he picked me up at the bus station, he offered his arm and opened the car door for me. Yes, Dee, you taught him right. You can be proud of him." She gave Dolores a nod, as if that settled the question of his innocence too. After the nod, she rubbed her temples.

"I shouldn't make quick movements," she said. "It's my headaches. They're getting better since I came to Copper Mill, but they haven't gone away. Gary said we had a gas leak at the house. That's one of the reasons I'm visiting. He sent me to visit Dee while he fixes it. He's so thoughtful."

Trixie leaned back, covered her forehead with the back of her hand, and closed her eyes. Kate couldn't help but wish she wouldn't brag about her son in the presence of a distraught Dolores.

"Well, I'll leave so you can rest," Kate said. Impulsively, she leaned over and gave Dolores a brief hug. "Please call me if I can do anything to help. You know we're praying for you."

"Yes, thank you. That means a lot to me." Dolores stood when Kate got up. "Thank you for the cookies too. I haven't had much of an appetite, but I do love chocolate-chip cookies."

She gave Kate a grateful smile and followed her to the door. "I believe my son is innocent, and I'm not going to let that sheriff or the busybodies around here say otherwise."

"Good. That's the spirit," Kate said.

As Kate walked to her car, Dolores stood in the doorway and watched her leave. Kate hadn't learned anything to help Skip, but at least his mother seemed to be holding up, she thought, glad that she'd come to visit and that Trixie was there to help.

KATE STOPPED AT THE MERCANTILE on the way home. She picked up a couple of food items, then wandered over to the cards and gifts. She found a cute encouragement card, then looked over the candles, small figurines, and plaques with witty sayings. None of them appealed to her.

She passed them and found the stuffed animals. There was an assortment of dogs, cats, and teddy bears in all colors and sizes. Tucked in among them was a soft white lamb that begged to be held and cuddled. She picked it up. Yes, that would work perfectly. She found a pretty floral gift bag and bright yellow tissue paper that was sure to lift Wendy's spirits.

Kate was pleased to see Arlene Jacobs at the cash register. She glanced around. No customers behind her. She placed her items on the counter.

"Hi, Kate. How are you?" Arlene asked as she scanned the card and set it aside.

"Fine. I heard you started an exercise class in the multi-purpose room at Town Hall," Kate said.

"I did!" Arlene grinned. "It's just five of us, but I'm hoping to attract more ladies. Did you want to come?"

She didn't wait for Kate's reply but kept right on talking. "I'm looking for a babysitter too. We have a few ladies who can only come if they bring their kids. Most of the time, they play in the corner, so it's all right, but this week Prissy Ranken's son snuck out, and she had to go chase him down. She found him talking to some strange man in the lobby. Well, that scared her all right, so now we're looking for someone to help us with that."

Kate's heartbeat sped up at the mention of the stranger. Whoever it was could have returned later to steal the coin.

Arlene scanned the lamb. "Aw, that's cute. Is it for one of your grandkids?"

"Actually, it's for Wendy Hart. She's having a difficult pregnancy. She might want to join your class after the baby's born. Do you know her?"

"That'd be cool. I remember her from high school. She married Billy Hart. I'll give her a call."

"She's in the hospital until the baby comes. I'm sure she'd love a phone call there." Kate glanced around. Still no customers behind her. "Say, did you see anyone or notice anything unusual at Town Hall Wednesday? What about that strange man? Did you find out who he was?"

"No. Prissy didn't know him, and I didn't see him. Is this about the missing coin? I heard about it," Arlene said as she scanned Kate's credit card. "I know what they're saying about

Skip. I can't believe he would have taken it. I don't know where he went, but it must be important. He can be a little flaky, but I just can't imagine that he would steal."

"I don't think he did it either, and I want to prove it."

Arlene printed out the register receipt and handed it to Kate to sign. "There were the tourists. Must have been at least five or six people. They came in here yesterday all bundled up with jackets, gloves, and hats and heavy boots. One of the ladies asked if we had ready-made sandwiches for a picnic. I can't believe anyone would want to have a picnic in this weather."

She affected a shiver. Then her eyes grew wide. "They'd been to Town Hall and they were talking about the mines. Do you think one of them took it?"

"I'm sure they're just interested tourists," Kate said, although she wasn't at all sure. But she didn't want a rumor to start about people who might be innocent bystanders.

LATE SATURDAY AFTERNOON, Paul hefted a large black plastic bag into the back of his pickup truck on top of stacks of bundled newspapers, broken-down cardboard boxes, and a box of empty glass jars in every imaginable size and shape, ready for a trip to the transfer station just outside town. It amazed him how two people could accumulate so much clutter.

He swept away the remaining debris with a large push broom, then stood back and stared at the blank wall inside the garage. *Much better*, he thought with satisfaction.

He'd purchased several large plastic trash bins with tight lids and set them outside the garage door on the side of the house for recyclable trash, determined that this wall would remain clear until he could transform the small domain into a workbench that would be his private work space. Although he laid no claim to woodworking skills, he'd seen some projects that piqued his interest. Besides, a man needed a place to fix things.

Taking a lined yellow pad and mechanical pencil he'd picked up at the Mercantile, Paul leaned against the front of his Chevy pickup. Resting one foot on the bumper for balance, he started drawing lines, sketching a rough work area. He scratched out his first attempt, flipped the page back, and started again.

After several attempts, he ripped off the discards and tucked the pencil into his pocket. This wouldn't be as simple as he'd envisioned. He went inside the house.

Kate was in her studio. The door was open, and she was seated on a stool facing him, leaning over the table, wrapping foil strips around small pieces of glass. She made for a charming view—one he enjoyed watching. The overhead light shone down on her strawberry blonde hair, making it gleam. A few tendrils fell around her face as she concentrated on her work.

She didn't look up at his approach. He admired her concentration. When she focused on a task or a problem, the rest of the world practically disappeared from her peripheral vision. He cleared his throat. She glanced up over the top of her reading glasses, her lively brown eyes slowly refocusing. She smiled. He smiled back.

"I'm going to make a run to the transfer station, then stop at the Mercantile for a magazine. You need anything?"

Kate sat straighter on the stool and arched her back, rubbing a hand down her side to her waist. She looked off to the right, as if in thought, then shook her head. "Can't think of a thing. Thanks. What time is it?"

"Almost four o'clock."

"Goodness, I've lost all track of time. You'd better get going before they close." She set the piece of glass and copper foil down on the table and removed her glasses. "I'll start supper while you're gone."

"Take your time. I'll help you when I get back." He gave her a kiss as she moved past him.

She grinned and shook her finger at him. He laughed, feeling pretty spunky. Kate had a way of making him feel much younger than his sixty-two years. He grabbed his keys, whistling a tune as he headed for his truck.

He couldn't wait to start his project, and the clean garage cleared the way. He thought about his meeting with Tom. It seemed God had placed that young man in his line of vision for a purpose. Paul wanted to help, and he hoped Tom could give him some advice. That relationship could become mutually beneficial.

Chapter Nine

Sunday morning, when Paul invited the congregation to greet each other before worship time, Kate glanced around, hoping to see Sheena and her husband, but the young waitress wasn't there.

Kate greeted Abby Pippins, asking if she had any news on Wendy. Abby only knew that she was still in the hospital on bed rest. Their conversation was cut short when Sam Gorman played the introduction to "Blest Be the Tie That Binds" on the organ.

Kate joined the choir on stage, her alto voice ringing out with the melody. She managed to sing on key most of the time, which Renee Lambert insisted made her perfect for the church choir. She wasn't so sure, but she could make a joyful noise, and that she did with enthusiasm.

Kate wasn't necessarily surprised that the waitress hadn't come to the service. She had no idea whether the young woman had ever attended church, and showing up in a strange church where she didn't know anyone would take a lot of courage. Still, Kate had hoped she could introduce Sheena and her husband to several younger couples in town. She added a silent prayer for the young couple and the pregnant young woman in the hospital and for Skip, while Paul prayed from the pulpit for those in the congregation suffering from any number of ailments and trials.

After Paul's message, as the organ rang out the postlude and the church became noisy with people leaving and chatting, Kate hurried out to the narthex, where Paul had already taken his place greeting parishioners as they left. She shook hands, hugged, and chatted with friends as they passed by.

Sam Gorman ended the organ postlude and joined Kate and Paul outside in the bright sunshine of the chilly late January day. The men arranged to meet midweek for lunch, as they often did. Kate watched Sam lumber down the steps and marveled that a man with such bulky, clumsy hands and labored movements could play such beautiful music on the organ.

"May I take you out for dinner?" Paul asked, smiling down at Kate and interrupting her thoughts. "I need to make a visit to the hospital. I thought you might want to come along."

"As a matter of fact, I do." Kate smiled at her husband. "There's a young woman I want to visit."

DINNER AT THE HOSPITAL CAFETERIA consisted of meat loaf with baked fingerling potatoes, coleslaw, and black-eyed peas.

"I'm stuffed," Kate told Paul as they walked to the elevator. "Don't expect any supper tonight."

"How about popcorn and an old movie?" he suggested. They occasionally enjoyed renting classics and curling up on the couch with a quilt.

"You're on." Kate thought about the people they were here to visit. "Let's stop at maternity first so I can deliver my gift."

"Lead the way."

They got directions to Wendy Hart's room at the nurse's station. As they approached the doorway, they could hear a football game on the television.

A young woman who appeared to be in her early twenties sat in the bed with her head propped up. Her dark hair was pulled up with a clip, but it stuck out in every direction. The large lump beneath the covers revealed her advanced pregnancy. She looked thoroughly bored.

In a chair near the foot of the bed, a young man with several days' growth of beard and shaggy hair was slouched, staring at the television above him. The announcer yelled about a spectacular run down the field. The young man sat straighter and started pounding the air with his fists.

"Go, go, go, *awww* . . ." His voice trailed off. "So close," he grumbled.

Kate tapped on the open door.

"Wendy?" Kate asked.

"Yeah?" The girl's eyes lit up when Kate held up the pretty present.

"I'm Kate Hanlon. This is my husband, Paul. We're from Copper Mill, from Faith Briar Church."

"Oh, yeah. I used to go there when I was in school," she said. "Come on in. That's my husband, Billy," she said, indicating the young man.

Paul stepped forward and held out his hand. "Hi, Billy," he said.

Billy looked up at the interruption and started to stand, taking Paul's hand.

"Don't get up," Paul said. "Who's playing?" He went to the other side and pulled up a chair to sit next to Billy.

"Tennessee and Houston. We're behind by one lousy point. Missed a first down by inches on that last play."

An instant bond formed as the two men discussed the game, leaving Kate free to talk to the young woman. She moved near the head of the bed.

"Our church is praying for you," Kate said, handing Wendy the present.

"Really? That's so nice. My mom always prayed for people. She used to tell me God always hears and answers, even if it isn't the answer we want. I didn't know anyone there would remember me . . . or care," she added. "I've been praying lately, but it doesn't seem like God's listening. Maybe he is." Wendy blinked away moisture in her eyes, but Kate noticed her emotional reaction.

Wendy untied the ribbon on the bag and opened it. She pulled out the card and set it aside, then pulled out the cuddly white lamb.

"*Oooh*, he's so cute," she gushed. She held it up to her cheek, then tucked it close to her neck. "Thank you. That's so sweet. My baby will love it." She patted her tummy.

Kate chuckled. "Meanwhile, you can cuddle with it," she said. "My daughters still love their stuffed animals, so I thought this might cheer you up."

"Yeah." Her face fell, but then she looked up and smiled. "I'm not used to sitting around doing nothing. I hope this baby comes soon."

Kate sensed that Wendy needed someone to talk with, so she pulled up a chair that was in the corner and sat beside the young woman. "When are you due?"

"Not for six weeks. *Six whole weeks.* I don't know what I'd do if Billy wasn't here. Thank goodness they let him come." She pursed her lips as if she'd said something wrong.

"Is Billy taking time off work?" Kate asked, imagining that must be a hardship on their finances.

"No. He lost his job."

"I'm sorry to hear that. That must be causing you concern," Kate said, giving Wendy an understanding smile. "We'll pray for him to find a new job. My husband can ask around and see if there are any openings."

"It'll take a miracle," Wendy said.

She studied Kate for a moment, as if sizing her up. Kate had found that people often opened up to her because of her role as a pastor's wife. Especially if they believed in the power of prayer. Evidently Wendy decided she would trust Kate because she leaned her head closer.

"Billy got caught driving without a license. He didn't tell his boss that he'd lost his license 'cause he had to make deliveries sometimes. He doesn't mean to do things wrong, but he keeps getting in trouble. He had some unpaid tickets, and he hadn't renewed the car registration, so he was in jail when I started having trouble. If the judge hadn't signed a release order, he'd still be there." Wendy's shoulders slumped. "We couldn't afford bail. I don't know how we're going to afford a baby."

A thought flashed into Kate's mind. "Was Billy in jail in Copper Mill by any chance?" she asked Wendy.

"Yeah. Skip—he's a friend of Billy's from way back—he went and talked to the judge, and the judge agreed to let Billy out until after the baby's born. Eventually he has to go see the judge and have a hearing. I hope he can find another job, but it doesn't look good. Who wants to hire someone who might have to go to jail?"

Kate was astounded by the news. How did Sheriff Roberts not know about the release order? She tried to keep the conversation focused on the young woman in front of her before her mind ran off in a million directions.

"I see your point," Kate said. "Where did he work?"

"At the lumberyard here in Pine Ridge. He's good at working on cars too. He worked at Bernie's Body Shop when he got out of high school, but Bernie couldn't afford to pay him much. Not enough to support a family." Wendy sighed.

"Has he gone back to talk to Bernie?"

"No. He's kind of proud, you know." Wendy absentmindedly petted the little white lamb as if it was a kitten on her lap. "I've been kind of worried. I don't know how soon I can go back to work, and then I'll have to find a babysitter unless Billy stays home. It's almost not worth it. Child care will eat up most of my paychecks. I'll hardly clear enough to pay the rent."

"I agree with your mother. God is listening to all of our prayers, and something will turn up," Kate said, patting Wendy's arm. "For now, just do as the doctors say. They know what you and the baby need. And I'll come back to visit you again."

Wendy reached out and grabbed Kate's hand. "Thanks. For the lamb and for coming to see me. After the baby's born, I'll come to church." She blushed. "I mean that. I want my baby to be raised in church, even if I haven't been good about coming."

Kate smiled gently. "Having children makes us examine our priorities a little more closely sometimes. We'd love to have you come to church, and we have a wonderful nursery for the baby." She scribbled her phone number on a piece of paper and handed it to Wendy. "Call me if you need anything."

"I will. I was lying here wishing my mom was here, and then you walked in. I want to see her, but I don't want to tell her about Billy going to jail and losing his job."

"Does she know about your pregnancy?"

"Oh yes. She's excited about becoming a grandma. She's coming when the baby's due, but that's not for weeks. I didn't tell her I'm having trouble. She'd just worry."

"Mothers do that. But I can say that as a mother, I'd want to know. She'll want to be praying for you at least."

Wendy chewed on her lip. "You're right. I'll call her. Billy might not like it. They don't get along very good."

"Maybe it'll be better this time." Kate patted Wendy's hand, then stood. "We need to go, but I'll be back, and I'll be praying for you and the baby and Billy."

"Thanks." Wendy hugged the lamb and smiled at Kate.

"NICE KIDS," PAUL SAID as they walked down the hall to visit the next patient on Paul's list. "Billy asked if he could come talk to me. He said he wants to get his life straightened up for his baby."

Kate tucked her hand through Paul's arm. "I'm so glad. Wendy's worried about their future. She's been praying and was glad people are praying for her. And Paul, here's the strangest piece of the puzzle: Billy is the escaped prisoner."

Paul stopped abruptly and turned to Kate. "I guess he's in more serious trouble than I thought."

"But he didn't escape like Sheriff Roberts thinks. Skip went and talked to the judge, and the judge signed a release order. Evidently Skip didn't tell the sheriff."

"That's not good. But at least we don't have a fugitive on our hands."

"Well, only if you don't count Skip. Sheriff Roberts thinks Skip is a fugitive. I need to call him and tell him about Billy. That clears Skip of at least one charge."

They walked arm in arm down the corridor. An hour later, they were in the car headed for Copper Mill. Kate took out her cell phone and dialed the sheriff's main office phone. She got a recorded message.

"Sheriff, it's Kate Hanlon. I found your prisoner, and he is not an escapee. The judge signed an order for his release. Call me for more information." Kate hung up and turned toward Paul. "I hope that makes him doubt the rest of his suspicions about Skip."

He glanced over at her. "I hope so too, but I wouldn't count on it."

It was just cool enough in the house to cuddle beneath a quilt. While Kate popped kettle corn, Paul built a fire in the river-rock fireplace in the corner of the living room.

Kate set the large bowl of popcorn on the coffee table and settled onto the couch.

"What's it going to be?" Paul asked, holding three DVD cases. "Western, romance, or adventure?"

"Western," Kate said, figuring that was likely to include all three categories.

Paul grinned. He opened a case and removed the DVD, then handed the case to Kate while he put the DVD in the player.

She looked at the cover. "*McLintock!*" she read out loud. "I should have known you'd pick a John Wayne movie. And I love Maureen O'Hara. This should be good." She filled a small bowl with popcorn and sat back.

Paul joined her. They spread the quilt over their laps, and he clicked on the movie.

They'd just gotten to the scene where McLintock's estranged wife arrived from the East, when the phone rang. Kate tried to ignore it, but Paul put the movie on pause and got up to answer it.

He came back into the living room with the cordless phone. "It's Sheriff Roberts," he said quietly.

Kate took the phone. "Hold the movie for me," she said, taking the phone and walking into the kitchen. "Good evening, Sheriff," Kate said into the phone. She settled into one of the chairs at the table.

"Evening. I got your message," Sheriff Roberts said. "What's this about my missing prisoner?"

"I met him this afternoon at the hospital. His wife is a patient in maternity. Skip released Billy Hart Thursday morning on the judge's orders." Kate cradled the phone against her shoulder. "Evidently Skip took it upon himself to ask for the release so Billy could be with his wife. I guess he didn't let you know."

"This is the first I've heard of it. He should have consulted me before he took action on his own." Sheriff Roberts made a sound deep in his throat. "But if this gets confirmed, it does prove he's not out chasing an escaped prisoner."

"True," Kate said, realizing he was right.

Billy's presence at the hospital shot that theory out the window for good. She was glad Billy hadn't broken out of jail. The young man had enough problems to deal with without adding a jailbreak to his list of infractions. But that destroyed one possible alibi for Skip.

"I appreciate the information, Kate. I'll let you get back to your evening," he said.

"Thanks, Sheriff. At least in the movie we're watching, John Wayne is guaranteed to get the bad guys."

She heard a snort at the other end of the phone. "Good night, Kate," he said.

She hung up and went back into the living room. Paul clicked Play on the remote. She settled back to watch the movie, but she couldn't get Skip and Wendy and Billy out of her mind. Sheena and her husband were there too. These young people had problems just living from one day to the next. They needed to see they had purpose and possibilities beyond their struggles.

Kate thought back on her childhood. She'd grown up in a Christian home with supportive, encouraging parents, but she hadn't found personal faith until college. And then she found many teachers and mentors who helped her mature. She thanked God that her children had all come to know the Lord, but that didn't mean they had fewer struggles; it just meant they took refuge in God's strength and hope and wisdom.

The movie shut off. Kate blinked. Had it finished? She wasn't even aware of it.

"Where are you, Katie?" Paul asked softly, leaning against her.

Kate chuckled. "Is the movie already over?"

"No, but I couldn't concentrate. Too much heavy thinking going on next to me. You're frowning." He took hold of her hand, entwining his fingers in hers. "What's wrong?"

"I was just thinking about Skip, which led to thoughts about Wendy and Billy, and then Sheena and Tom, and then of course our own children."

"Of course. A natural progression. So much potential and life ahead of them, but so many struggles."

"Exactly. I'm so glad our children all have strong faith, but they're so far away. What happens when they need us? When they need a shoulder to cry on and someone to listen and give them good advice? I pray for them, but I feel so helpless sometimes."

"I know. I feel that way too, but then I remember what Paul said in 2 Corinthians: 'My grace is sufficient for you, for my power is made perfect in weakness.' I take great comfort in that. And I take great comfort that I have you."

Kate smiled back. "And I have you. The Lord knew I needed someone rock solid. But I also had mentors in college and all the wise older women in our church in San Antonio. They taught me so much." Her eyes widened, then she started laughing.

"What?" Paul asked, looking confused, as if the subject had changed and he'd missed his cue.

"It just occurred to me. I *am* the older woman now. Oh my. I don't feel old. Can you imagine how we look to those young people?" Then she sobered. "Have we been dumped into these young peoples' lives to be the old, wise mentors?"

Paul rubbed his chin. "Very possible. But you don't look old Katie."

She nudged Paul playfully. "And you might be a bit nearsighted, but I suspect that youth is in the eye of the beholder. I hope our kids have wise older mentors in their lives."

Paul put his arm around her shoulders and gave her a squeeze. "I have no doubt they do. God doesn't leave us to struggle on our own." He hugged her close and leaned his head against hers. "Now, shall we watch the rest of the movie?"

"Mm-hmm," she murmured, cuddling against his side, loving his warmth and strength.

He clicked the Play button, and the movie came back to life on the television screen. Too bad life wasn't as easy as controlling a DVD. She would solve everyone's problems with the click of a button. At the least, she'd love to put this whole problem on pause until she could find the real culprit and clear Skip.

Chapter Ten

Kate walked into the Copper Mill Branch of Mid-Cumberland Bank and Trust at nine o'clock Monday morning. Evelyn Cline was waiting on a customer, but her twin sister Georgia's teller window was open. The elderly woman's eyes lit up when Kate approached her window.

"Morning, Kate," Georgia said. "How are you today?"

"Good as I can be," Kate said, smiling. "You're looking fine today."

Georgia sat up tall and beamed. "Thank you. What can I do for you?"

"I have a deposit." Kate slid the deposit across the counter. She couldn't help hearing the conversation at the next window. The customer spoke quite clearly, mentioning the robbery at Town Hall to Evelyn. Evelyn said it was a shame.

Georgia shook her head and made a tsk-tsk sound. She looked up at Kate. "What do you make of the robbery?"

"I really can't say," Kate replied, which could have meant anything.

She knew the Cline sisters loved to be in the know, and she'd gained a reputation for solving mysteries, but she didn't want to encourage a rumor.

As her customer left, Evelyn leaned toward them, shaking her head in a way that sent her bluish white hair bobbing. Her wide eyes looked enormous through her wire-rimmed glasses. "Our grandfather had one of the original coins. They're rare, you know."

Kate's ears perked up. "Are they," she said, more a comment than a question.

Georgia frowned at her sister, a look Kate interpreted as a warning. As the eldest by a few minutes, Georgia had a tendency to boss her sister around. Kate thought it a bit odd that she wanted to stifle her sister's comments. The pair were notorious gossips in Copper Mill.

"They only made coins for the mine owners and major investors, plus one they presented to the governor and one to the town in a special memorial celebration," Georgia explained.

"Oh yes," Evelyn chimed in, her eyelashes fluttering. "Remember Grandfather telling us about it when we were little? They had a band and dancing and a box social. It must have been a grand affair."

"That's not the point," Georgia said, giving her sister a reproving glance. She turned back to Kate. "Grandfather was an engineer for the mine, and he did well investing in the company. He even hired George Barber from Knoxville to build our home."

Kate hadn't heard of George Barber, but the pride in Georgia's voice indicated he was a builder of some renown.

"Then the Depression hit and the mines closed," Evelyn injected, clasping her hands together dramatically. "Grandfather sold his coin and other valuables to save the house. We've been looking to buy one of the coins for years, but we'll never be able to." She stared at the ceiling as if she were off in another world or time.

"We heard Skip Spencer took the coin. The sheriff needs to find him before he sells it to the highest bidder," Georgia said.

"What makes you think Skip has it?" Kate asked.

"The evidence is plain," Georgia said. "He absconded with the coin and enough money to move to Florida and start a new life."

"Florida?" Kate asked, her interest piqued.

"He purchased a Florida map at the Quik Stop gas station," Georgia said. "Everyone is talking about it. Of course, we did our duty and reported what we know to the sheriff."

"Of course."

Nothing the sisters said proved Skip's guilt or innocence. Their rambling gave Kate a couple of avenues to explore, however.

Georgia completed Kate's deposit transaction, and Kate took the receipt, slipping it into her handbag.

"Thanks," she said. "It's certainly nippy out, isn't it?" She flipped the tail of her wool scarf with its fringe and long silken threads around her neck. "I doubt I'll ever acclimate to this weather. I love the winter clothing, though."

"Give me a good wool tweed any day," Georgia replied. She nodded toward her sister. "Evelyn prefers spring and summer."

The two sisters looked as alike as could be. Especially when they dressed similarly, which they did often.

"I must run," Kate said, stepping away. "Have a nice day," she added before she turned to leave.

"Deputy Spencer knows the value of that coin," Georgia said as an afterthought. "I told him about our search once."

Kate froze. As the eldest twin, Georgia knew how to get in the last word to the most effect.

KATE WENT STRAIGHT TO THE LIBRARY from the bank. Livvy was busy, so Kate went upstairs and found an unused computer and logged onto the Internet.

First she checked her e-mail. A list of incoming messages appeared. She was disappointed that there weren't any e-mails from Coppercop or Jjohns, but there was a note from the coin dealer. Excited, she opened the message.

> *Dear Kate,*
>
> *I've researched your coin. The Superior Mint and Casting Company of Charlotte, NC, operated from 1815 until 1863. It closed during the Civil War and never reopened. The private mint is noted for producing fine gold coins and medallions that have become prized collectors' coins and museum pieces. I found a coin that fits your description in my antique references. Without seeing your coin, it's impossible to establish exact value. Only thirty of the coins were minted. Based on its origin and rarity, I'd estimate its value in the range of $5,000.00–$12,000.00, depending upon its condition. I recommend taking it to a qualified coin appraiser to determine its exact value.*

Kate sent off a thank-you response, then stared at the estimated value, amazed. Evelyn Cline had hinted at its worth. Georgia had shot her sister a warning glance. How desperate were they to replace their grandfather's coin? They couldn't afford to purchase one, even if they could find one for sale. Would they resort to theft? Kate couldn't imagine them going to such lengths. Their positions at the bank enabled them to handle a lot of money. The bank did track deposits and withdrawals carefully, however.

Kate had considered her previous attempt to follow someone else's word searches to find the coin. She tried a different tactic, typing "old commemorative medallions" into the computer's search engine. Pages and pages of references came up for a category called exonumia, which referred to coinlike tokens and medals that weren't legal currency.

Scrolling through the search results, she found a link to medal art that brought up casting, striking, and repoussé tokens and medals. She found some beautiful pictures of Civil War medals and Indian peace medals, but they weren't what she was looking for.

As she clicked through different Web listings, she found a site for stolen exonumia and checked it out. The Copper Mill coin wasn't listed, and there weren't any others like it. She jotted down the site in case the sheriff or the mayor wanted to list the missing coin.

She checked out several auction sites, finding old mining medallions from California and Alaska and recent ones from Shanghai, but nothing copper from Tennessee or the Carolinas.

Typing in "copper mining coins and medallions" brought up a lot of cheap souvenir tokens.

Giving up, she logged off. As she started down the stairs, Livvy was coming up. She met Kate halfway and stopped on the steps.

"Are you leaving? I found out who was looking through our history books," Livvy said.

"Oh, good. I've been thinking about who it could have been. Was it the group from the hotel?"

Livvy nodded. "You never cease to amaze me, Kate. Yes, it was them. They asked about the mining history in the area. Seems they're part of a group that travels around the country visiting mines and mining museums."

"That would explain their interest." Kate didn't mention that they were also likely the people who conducted an Internet search for the missing coin before Kate. She didn't want to cast suspicion on them until she knew more.

"Did you find anything in the books?"

"I haven't had time to look. I was searching the Internet. I haven't found anything about our coin yet."

"I doubt if you'll find much in the books either. I believe there's just one account of the celebration and a copy of the same article that's in the display case."

"Which won't help us find the coin," Kate said. "I'll try again tomorrow. What are you doing today for lunch?"

"Nothing special."

"Good. Want to meet me at the diner? Eleven thirty?"

KATE ARRIVED AT THE COUNTRY DINER before Livvy. It was too cold to wait outside, so she went inside. She had to wait a few minutes to get a booth, even though it was early. She'd barely sat down when LuAnne Matthews plopped down next to her.

"Howdy, Kate darlin', how are you?" LuAnne's soft southern drawl strung out her words.

"Good. How are you?"

"Fine and dandy." LuAnne leaned on her elbow toward Kate as if to block out the rest of the customers. "Have you cleared Skip yet? That poor boy." She shook her head, tossing her bottle-red hair.

"Not yet," she said.

"You will. He might not be the brightest bulb on the Christmas tree, but I've always liked him. Treats me like a lady, you know? Even when I'm workin', he says 'yes, ma'am, no, ma'am, thank you, ma'am.' His mama taught him right."

She looked over her shoulder, then back at Kate. "I don't believe the rumors. I've been keepin' my ears open. Somebody knows who did it, and sooner or later they'll let something slip out. When they do, I'll let you know."

Kate had to smile. LuAnne seemed to think she was a supersleuth. "Thanks, LuAnne." Kate peered around her. "You seem to be really busy today. Is the new waitress here today? She seems like a nice girl."

"Sheena? Yeah, she's a sweetie. Works hard too. You want her to wait on your table?"

Kate nodded. "I met her last week when Paul and I came in. I just wanted to see how she's doing. Sometimes it's hard to settle into a new town, you know."

Just as LuAnne slipped out of the booth, Livvy arrived and slid into the seat across from Kate.

"Hi, LuAnne. Sorry I'm late, Kate."

"No problem," LuAnne answered for Kate. She gave Kate a wink. "I'll send Sheena over."

Kate gave Sheena a big smile as she approached. "Hi, Sheena. This is Livvy Jenner. She's the town librarian."

"Hi," Sheena said. She handed them each a menu. "Special

today is chicken-fried steak and mashed potatoes and gravy. Do you know what you want, or shall I give you a few minutes?"

"I'm ready," Livvy said, and Kate nodded in agreement. "I'll have a Po' Boy," Livvy said.

Kate was tempted, but she resisted and ordered a chef salad. She watched Sheena hurry off with their orders. She was a bit disappointed. She'd wanted to have some kind of dialogue with Sheena, but the young waitress acted preoccupied.

"Maybe she can chat when she comes back," Livvy said, observant as always.

Although Livvy was younger than Kate, the two were kindred spirits. Their friendship had clicked from the moment they met. Livvy's kind heart, her probing mind, and her love of anything mysterious or puzzling made her the perfect companion to Kate's inquisitive nature. Even more important, Kate trusted her discretion and heart completely, and that meant the world.

"So, what's up?" Livvy asked. "Have you found the coin burglar?"

Kate shook her head. "I have a few ideas to explore. I did learn that the coin is rare and valuable. Georgia and Evelyn said their grandfather owned one before the Depression."

"Unless people threw them away as junk, there must be others around. That's why I can't understand anyone stealing it. Exchanging the coin for a car-wash token in its place seems more like a prank than a serious robbery."

"You're saying someone could have used the key, put a token in place of the coin, then replaced the key as a practical joke?"

"It's possible. High-school kids are always pulling tricks. I wonder if James or Justin has heard anything. I'll ask them."

Livvy's boys were teenagers. If someone had pulled a prank, word would get around.

"If someone took the coin as a joke, they'd have a hard time getting past the reserve deputy to return it," Kate said.

"You mean Hugh Martin? He's sharp. He worked highway patrol around here for years. No one got away with speeding or anything else. And he's not gullible like Skip."

Sheena came with their orders. Livvy complimented her necklace. "Mixing shells with the beads reminds me of a tropical island. It's lovely."

"Thanks. It cheers me up on such a cold day," Sheena said, clearly pleased.

"Is this one that you made?" Kate asked.

"Yeah." She straightened up but didn't look like she was about to retreat. "I like to play around with jewelry. I make some of my own beads."

"You're very talented," Kate said. "How are you and Tom doing?"

Sheena sighed. She glanced toward the other tables, making sure she wasn't needed. Then she turned back to Kate and Livvy. "He can't find any work," she said. "It's not right. He's so talented. He's working on the place, fixing it up for the landlord." She leaned closer to Kate. "Place is a dump," she said in a quiet voice that Kate barely heard. "The landlord should be paying *us* to stay there. We've chased mice out and cleaned it up." She rolled her eyes. "We'll find a better place as soon as Tom gets a job."

"I hope that's soon."

"Something's gotta give, or we'll have to move again."

The front door opened, and a group of men came in.

"I gotta get back to work. Wave at me if you need anything."

Sheena grabbed a stack of menus, then followed the group to a table. Kate watched the men file past. She recognized Doug Campbell, the head of Campbell Construction, and two of the young men who worked for him. She glanced at their feet. They all had on work boots with heavy soles. Most were well worn and scuffed. One pair looked brand-new. Kate sighed. If she tried to check all the work boots in town to match the treads at Town Hall, she'd never find the thief, if indeed a man in work boots had stolen the coin at all.

"Cute girl," Livvy said. "Kind of reminds me of a flower child, with her long skirt and beads and long hair. I gather she just moved to Copper Mill."

Kate had to switch mental gears to realize that Livvy was watching Sheena. "Yes. I hope her husband can find work. With winter here, I doubt there's much construction going on. I think a lot of folks are struggling to find employment. I met another young man the other day without a job. Do you know Billy Hart?"

"Oh yes, I remember Billy. I had to evict him from the library several times when he was in high school. He was a clown. He'd get the other kids giggling with his antics." Livvy grinned. Livvy's own boys were well behaved but not immune to cutting up once in a while. They *were* teenagers. Besides, Livvy was by nature a cheerful person. "I heard about his wife, Wendy, from the prayer chain. Is she doing all right?"

"Seems to be," Kate said. "She's bored being in the hospital.

Abby told me Wendy used to go to Faith Briar. Do you remember her?"

"Yes. She's a quiet girl. Pretty. She and Billy Hart were inseparable, and her parents weren't happy about it. He's a likable kid but doesn't have much ambition. He went to church with Wendy's family once, and he sat in the pew and fidgeted through the entire service." Livvy chuckled. "'Course, my boys have been known to do that. Wendy's mother had problems with arthritis, so her parents decided to move to a drier climate."

Sheena came back to clear the plates and bring the bill.

"We're looking forward to having you come to dinner tomorrow night," Kate said.

"Us too," Sheena said. "You're our first invitation." She smiled shyly and said good-bye.

Livvy fished a ten-dollar bill out of her purse and put it on the table, paying for her lunch and leaving a generous tip. "I'd better get back to work."

ON HER WAY HOME, Kate stopped at the pharmacy. She was low on calcium supplements, and she wanted to talk to Fred Cowan, since he'd been to Town Hall around the time the coin had disappeared.

Ashland Street was torn up between the veterinary clinic and the pharmacy. A tall pile of dirt and pavement pieces, dusted lightly with snow, stood beside a large hole, cordoned off by bright yellow sawhorses with blinking orange lights on top. One lane remained open to get through to the pharmacy and Willy's Bait and Tackle across the street.

As Kate parked her car, the pharmacy door opened and a man stepped out—the same man she'd encountered going into

Town Hall on Thursday. She noticed he wore the same heavy work boots and green jacket he'd worn before. He glanced over his shoulder at the store, then took a pipe out of his jacket pocket.

As Kate walked toward the door, he took out a match-book and tore off a match, then he turned toward her as he struck the match and lit the pipe. The red and yellow match-book cover was bright against the steely sky. It looked vaguely familiar, but he slipped it back in his pocket before Kate could take a good look. He caught her staring, turned, and walked around the corner of the building without a smile, a nod, or any kind of acknowledgment. *Odd*, she thought. Did he not recognize her?

Inside, Kate saw two of the women who'd been with the man at the Country Diner. They were looking for something down one of the aisles.

Kate found the supplements she wanted and took them to the pharmacy window. Fred stood behind the counter, filling a prescription.

"Afternoon, Kate. Be with you in a minute."

"No hurry," Kate said. "What's going on in the street? They've sure made a mess out there."

"Don't I know it," Fred said, giving her a wry grin. "Not good for business, I tell you. January's bad enough without an obstacle course to get here. 'Course that robbery at Town Hall really livened things up. Everyone who comes in here wants to talk about it." Fred's bushy mustache curled over his upper lip when he pursed his lips. "I heard you discovered the coin was missing."

"I stopped in to talk to Skip," Kate said, not volunteering any more information.

Fred looked up from what he was doing. "Did you talk to him? I heard he disappeared."

"He wasn't there when I went in."

Kate heard the two ladies talking as they came to stand behind her. She stepped out of the way. "Go ahead. I'm not in a hurry," she said, giving them a smile. "Are you enjoying your visit to Copper Mill?"

"Oh yes," the shorter woman said.

Kate thought she might be the wife of the man outside. They'd been together at the diner.

"It's colder than we expected. I haven't been here since I was a teenager." She held out her hand to Kate. "I'm Eloise Henley. My uncle lives in town. Maybe you know him. Joshua Parsons?"

"Kate Hanlon." Kate shook her hand. "I know your uncle," she said. "I sometimes bring him meals from our church's food program."

"Oh, good." Eloise laughed. "You're just the person I want to talk to, then. Uncle Joshua has some special dietary needs. Perhaps I could talk to you sometime about adjusting his diet?"

"Sure," Kate said. "If nothing else, I can make sure everyone who volunteers for our Faith Freezer Program knows about the dietary restrictions. You're staying at the Hamilton Springs Hotel, aren't you? Our church is right next door, and we prepare the meals at the house next to it. Why don't you stop by some time?"

"Yes. I can come on Wednesday afternoon, if that works for you. Tomorrow we're going to drive the Old Copper Road down through the Ocoee River Gorge." She crossed her arms over her chest. "I wish it were warmer so we could walk around more. We should have waited until summertime to come down here. It's as cold here as Connecticut."

"We're having unusually cold temperatures, aren't we Fred?"

"Yes indeed." He gave Kate a wink.

"How long will you be in town?" Kate asked.

"Another week. If it warms up, we'll go rock hunting. My uncle promised to tell my husband where we can find some good copper ore and maybe some other gemstones. I collect agates."

"I hope you find some good stones."

"Me too. Well, I'd better get going. Griff will wonder what's keeping us," Eloise said.

Kate wondered if the woman's husband had other things on his mind. "I'll see you at the Faith Freezer House Wednesday afternoon, then. Say about one thirty?"

"Yes. I'll be there."

The two women paid for their purchases and left.

After the door closed behind them, Fred chuckled. "I wouldn't want to be digging around in this cold." He began to ring up Kate's purchase. "You know, Skip used to run deliveries for me when he was a teenager." He reached for the bottle of calcium and scanned it. "I trusted him with prescriptions for some of our old people, and he never let me down."

Fred pushed a button on his register and told Kate the total. "Skip wouldn't take the town's coin. He knows how much it means to people around here," he said as he slipped Kate's purchases into a plastic bag.

"I agree. Any idea who would? Have you seen anyone suspicious around?"

Fred shook his head. "I've thought about it. I didn't see anyone acting strange when I went to Town Hall, and I can't imagine someone around here would take it. A numismatist came to town a few years back, wanting to examine the coin." Fred chuckled again. "The mayor told him in no uncertain terms that he could look but not touch. The man protested around town to everyone who would listen. Stirred up a lot of interest at the time."

"Do you remember what he looked like? Could he have come back and stolen it?" Kate asked.

"I haven't seen him since then. And believe me, I'd remember if he showed up. He was real short and walked with a swagger. Reminded me of that actor Danny DeVito." Fred shook his head. "No, he hasn't been around. That was a long time ago. If he'd intended to steal it, he'd have done it a long time ago."

Kate hadn't seen anyone around town like Fred described. No help there. She thanked Fred and left.

As Kate walked to her car, stepping carefully to avoid the mud, Steve Smith came out of Willy's Bait and Tackle across the street. He saw Kate and waved, then crossed to his car. Kate noticed he was wearing heavy work boots very much like the tourist. She thought about the matchbook she'd seen the man use. It seemed familiar. She wished she could have gotten a closer look.

Chapter Eleven

First thing Tuesday morning, Kate made a trip to the gas station. She needed fuel for both her Honda and her mystery.

She topped off the gas in her car, then went inside to pay. The smells of coffee, hot dogs, and pizza mingled together.

"Just gas today?" Wilma Davis, the middle-aged assistant manager, asked. She had a pen sticking out of her hair above her ear.

Kate glanced around. A younger man was stocking shelves. Back by the refrigerated section, a child was begging a couple of young women for a soda. Kate didn't see anything she needed.

"That's it. Thanks, Wilma. How has business been lately?"

"Pretty good. Having a little notoriety hasn't hurt."

"I can imagine. People love a scandal. I saw Deputy Spencer roar out of here Thursday morning. Must have been his last stop before he left town."

"Sure was. He comes in every morning, you know. Buys three donuts. Well, he did, before he disappeared. Funny business. He was in a terrible rush that morning. Spent a couple of minutes looking around for something. Acted real agitated. He finally asked me where the maps were. He grabbed a Florida map, a couple of bags of chips, a ham-and-cheese sandwich, and a six-pack of sodas. He took out a huge wad of cash, then he dropped it and had to scramble to pick up the money."

Wilma shook her head as Kate handed her a twenty for the gas. "He was muttering under his breath. Couldn't make out what he was saying, but he looked kind of wild-eyed, if you know what I mean. He paid me, then took off. Jumped in his truck and peeled out like he was on his way to a fire. Didn't even take his change. Left a dollar and eighty cents sitting on the counter. Enough for his usual donuts and then some."

Wilma opened the register and slipped Kate's money into the till. "I've always thought he was a nice guy." She shrugged. "Guess I was wrong. Not surprising. I always did fall for the wrong men." She shoved the drawer closed.

"When I heard about the robbery," Wilma continued, "I just put two and two together. I mean, it's not rocket science. I watch those detective shows and crime-scene shows. I don't have any hard-and-fast evidence, but the circumstantial evidence is airtight, if you ask me. People get sent to prison on less. Coincidences like that don't happen in real life."

"He could have been hurrying for any number of reasons," Kate said diplomatically.

"Could have been, but I doubt it."

Kate thanked Wilma and walked back to her car, more discouraged than when she'd arrived.

Skip, you've stepped in a hornet's nest this time, and I don't know how you're going to get out. Why did you take off in such a hurry? she wondered as she drove away from the service station. *Why did you withdraw all your money? What is going on?*

"Lord, what am I going to do? Everything points to Skip. Am I wrong?" she prayed out loud as she drove. "I just can't believe he took that coin. He loves the law and swore to uphold it. What could possibly happen that would make him change his mind? What am I missing?"

AFTER LUNCH, KATE RETURNED TO TOWN to talk to Gertie at Town Hall. She'd tried calling the cleaning lady and had left messages, but Gertie hadn't returned her calls.

A sign in the lobby warned of wet floors. *Good*, Kate thought. *She's here.*

She walked down the hall, looking in offices for Gertie. A door opened. Gertie came out, saw Kate, pivoted around, and went back into the room, shutting the door. Kate reached for the doorknob. The door jerked open, wrenching the knob out of her hand.

Kate stood eye to eye with Gertie Crowe. The woman was her height, younger, Kate guessed, but it was hard to tell. She looked tired. Her light brown hair was held back with a large red clip. Her hazel eyes didn't blink as she looked at Kate, who quickly composed herself and smiled.

"Hi, Gertie, I'm Kate Hanlon. I've been trying . . ."

"I know who you are. Can't talk now. I'm working." Without a smile or any expression, Gertie marched past Kate and went down the hall, disappearing into the deputy's office.

Stunned, Kate watched her disappear. Obviously Gertie

didn't want to talk to her. That explained why she hadn't returned Kate's phone calls. Kate wondered why the woman was avoiding her. Frowning, she left the building. She'd have to do some checking on Gertie Crowe.

KATE PICKED OUT A PRETTY PASTEL Monet print scarf to wear for dinner. She wrapped a chain of tiny colored beads around the scarf and fastened it around her neck. It gave her celery green pants and knit top a touch of elegance, although that wasn't her aim. She knew Sheena loved necklaces and beads, and Kate hoped that her outfit would serve as a conversation piece.

Satisfied with her appearance, she returned to the kitchen. The roast, along with carrots, celery, onions, and a bowl of mashed potatoes were keeping warm in the oven.

Kate had debated whether to use her good china. She didn't want to seem pretentious, but she wanted the young couple to feel special. She decided on her everyday dishes. With a simple arrangement of evergreens and pinecones around a pillar candle, the table looked lovely.

Paul came in, his sleeves rolled up. He gave her a kiss. "Smells wonderful in here. How can I help?"

"Could you cut the roast? I'll toss the salad, then make the gravy. They should be here any minute."

Paul arranged a platter of sliced meat and vegetables and covered it with foil. He slid it into the oven just as the door-bell rang, then went to get the door.

Kate whisked the gravy as it came to a boil. She turned off the burner, covered the pan, and removed her apron just as Paul came back with Sheena and Tom.

"Welcome," Kate said, smiling broadly. "I'm so glad you could come."

Sheena looked lovely in a long gauzy skirt, boots, and a tie-dyed tunic. Her hair hung to the middle of her back in spiral curls, held away from her face by an intricate webbing of beads and gold tassels that jiggled and shimmered when she moved. Her gaze darted around the kitchen and dining area with apparent interest.

Tom had his hands in the pockets of his jeans, which were clean but faded and torn at the knees and several other places.

Watching them, Kate remembered her own days as a young wife. Living on an assistant pastor's salary had required squeezing every penny and exercising creativity, and her income as an executive assistant had been crucial to their existence. The usual marital challenges compounded when you couldn't find work and provide for your family.

Early in their marriage, with Kate's family nearby, she and Paul had the support of loved ones as well as the church. They had grown particularly close to one older couple at church. Kate had relied on their wisdom many times and admired their deep serenity and unshakable faith.

After Paul became senior pastor at Riverbend Community Church, they'd continued relationships with many of the young people who'd grown up in the church. She and Paul had mentored those couples through dating, marriage, and parenthood, but she'd never felt like that older, wiser woman before. Inside, she still felt like a young woman.

"Can I help?" Sheena asked.

"If you'd like to help me carry food to the table, we'll be ready to eat."

Kate handed her the bowl of salad. She knew Sheena was comfortable in a serving role and hoped that would put her at ease.

Sheena asked about salad dressing, then found Kate's homemade pear vinaigrette in the refrigerator and put it on the table. Soon they were seated at the table.

"Shall we pray?" Paul bowed his head and asked a blessing on their meal and time together.

Kate bowed her head. When Paul said "Amen," Kate opened her eyes as Tom and Sheena lifted their heads. She passed the bowl of mashed potatoes to Sheena.

"Please, help yourself." Kate started the salad around.

Paul took some meat and vegetables and passed the platter to Tom.

"This looks delicious," Tom said, taking a large serving.

Kate was glad. She had more than enough food, so she hoped he would load up.

"I talked to Sam Gorman at the Mercantile this morning," Paul said as he poured gravy over his potatoes and meat. "He worked in construction around here years ago, so I thought he'd know who to call. He gave me Doug Campbell's name. Campbell Construction has been in Copper Mill for years. Sam worked for Doug's father. He didn't know if they were hiring, but he gave me a phone number."

Paul fished a piece of paper out of his shirt pocket and handed it to Tom. "If he isn't hiring, he might know who is."

Tom took the paper, looked at it, then stuck it in his pocket. "Thanks. I'll call him."

"Tom's really talented," Sheena said, beaming at her husband.

"Getting on a local construction crew might open some doors for you," Kate commented. "You'd be able to meet people and show your expertise."

"Mm-hmm." Tom swallowed. "I put up some notices around town, but I haven't had any calls yet. Gives me time to work on the house, but the landlord doesn't want to spend any money, so I've had to find cheap materials. That's not easy."

"I don't imagine so," Kate said. "How are you doing, Sheena? Do you enjoy working at the Country Diner?"

"Yeah, I like it a lot, but it's just part-time, so I don't have regular hours. Loretta's been good to me, though, and the customers are all nice. There sure have been some disagreements about that coin robbery, though," she said, her brow creasing into tiny furrows. "Do you think that deputy took the coin? He seemed so nice when Tom and I talked to him at Town Hall. Remember Tom?"

Tom shrugged. "He's all right, I guess. Told us how to find places."

"Deputy Spencer is very friendly," Kate said. "I wouldn't pay attention to the rumors. I'm sure he's innocent. When did you meet him?"

"Right after we moved here," Sheena said. "We went to Town Hall to find out about getting our electricity turned on. The mayor himself gave us a tour of Town Hall. He told us that the town used to be rich because of all the mining around here, like that coin," she said, looking at Tom as if for confirmation. He was busy eating, but he nodded.

"Loretta said I could sell some of my beadwork at the diner," Sheena said, fingering the tassels that hung down over her ears. "Someday I hope to sell my jewelry to chic dress stores that sell, you know, retro and boho clothes in New York and Los Angeles."

Fortunately, Kate had a general idea what Sheena was talking about, since her daughter Rebecca loved the throwback Bohemian styles of the sixties and seventies. Copper Mill didn't quite fit that description. It was vintage, perhaps, but in a different sense.

"You could take some samples to stores in Pine Ridge," Kate said.

"That's a great idea." Sheena's eyes sparkled as she gave her curls a toss. The light caught the beads, sending shimmers of light dancing around the room and ceiling. "I have lots of pieces that I made before we moved here." She turned to her husband. "Tom, can you take me to Pine Ridge next week?" To Kate, she explained, "We just have the van. Usually Tom takes me to work, then uses it for business."

"I could take you," Kate said, eager to spend more one-on-one time with the young woman.

Sheena's face lit up. "Sweet. That'd be cool."

Tom wolfed down seconds. When Kate offered him more, he declined. "I'm stuffed. Sure was good."

"Maybe I should wait awhile to serve dessert," Kate said.

"That's a good idea. I'll take Tom out to see my project." Paul got up. He started to pick up his plate, but Kate shooed him away. He grinned. Kate knew he was excited to talk to Tom about his garage plans.

PAUL USHERED TOM OUT to the garage. He flipped on the overhead light, which wasn't very bright.

The garage was extra deep, allowing room for two cars,

with space in the front for a work area. The laundry area was off to the side. Paul's older model Chevy pickup took up quite a bit of room, but Kate's Honda Accord was compact.

"Here's where I want a workbench and some kind of shelving for tools and storage," Paul said, pointing out the wall he'd cleared. "I found this one design." He opened a magazine and pointed to a layout. "I don't need anything this fancy, though."

Tom pulled a tape measure off his belt. He stretched it out across the wall, then measured.

"You could easily build an eight-foot workbench and come out at least twenty-four inches if you want room for bins across the back for nuts and bolts and screws. Or you could go with a six-foot bench and have room for a tool cabinet at the end. They make some beauties."

"The six-footer should do. I don't have many tools, and I don't plan to do any complicated projects, but I'd like to putter around. Besides"—Paul grinned—"I need to give my kids something to give me besides ties."

"Ties?" Tom grimaced. "Yeah. Anything'd be better than that."

Paul chuckled at the look on Tom's face. He wondered if the young man had ever worn a tie. Perhaps at his wedding, but Paul guessed that he and Sheena might be too casual to go for a formal wedding.

"So, what do you think? Am I talking about a big project here?"

"Naw. You got something to write on?"

Paul handed Tom a clipboard with a graph-paper tablet and a pencil.

"Perfect." Tom leaned against the wall and started drawing. He took measurements and jotted figures on the paper. After a few minutes, he handed the tablet to Paul.

"Materials are simple," Tom said. "You want a good solid top. Beneath the counter, your base can be a wood or steel frame with a couple of shelves, or you can get prefab cabinets with or without doors. Same over the workbench. You can mount shelves or get cabinets. Either way, once you have the materials, the assembly shouldn't take long. A couple of days depending on what you decide on."

"Probably have to double the time if I do the work. I know you're looking for full-time employment Tom, but what would you charge to put something like this together?"

Tom rubbed his chin. He looked down at the floor, then up at Paul. "I need fifteen dollars an hour and flexible hours," he said.

"Sounds reasonable. How many hours do you estimate it'd take?"

"Maybe ten to fifteen."

Paul couldn't tell how badly Tom wanted work. He acted unconcerned, but Paul suspected he would take any job that came along. Paul knew he could do the project himself, but he also knew it would take all winter and a lot of frustration.

He nodded his head. "All right. Do you want the job?"

Tom let out a breath, then he smiled, a grin that slanted up, showing a dimple on one side of his face. "Yeah, I do."

Chapter Twelve

After the men went out to the garage, Sheena picked up a stack of dirty dishes and carried them to the sink.

She looked around the kitchen. "You don't have a dishwasher?"

Kate almost laughed at Sheena's shocked expression.

"No. The kitchen is too small. I don't mind. I'll rinse them off and wash them later."

"It may be small, but you've got great equipment," Sheena said, admiring Kate's state-of-the-art food processor and mixer. "I'll bet you do a lot of cooking."

"As much as possible. It's one of my hobbies. You'd think, since I'm not working, I'd spend more time in the kitchen, but even without a job, I still don't have as much free time as I did in San Antonio."

"You're from Texas? I should have guessed from your drawl. It's different."

"And here I thought I'd lost my accent."

"Oh no. I can hear it."

Kate carried a copper saucepan to the sink.

"I love your pans," Sheena said, looking at the rack of shiny copperware hanging from the ceiling. "They look like something on the fancy chef shows on television."

"I'd had my eye on the Mauviel copperware for years. I love cooking with copper. It cooks so evenly. I saved up for a long time to get these."

"Cool. I just ordered a really neat pan from the Food Network on TV. It's designed by one of those famous chefs. It's a grill and a smoker, deep fryer, roaster, and broiler all in one. It's going to make cooking so much easier. I only have two burners on the stove. Here, let me help with the dishes. My first job was washing dishes in Birmingham. They had a big commercial dishwasher, but I had to rinse everything and load it." She picked up a dishtowel. "I'll dry."

"All right." Kate filled the sink with hot water and dish soap. She lowered a plate into the water and started washing. She'd watched those cable food programs and seen the advertisements for the kinds of pans Sheena mentioned. They offered nice cookware and products, but most of them were expensive. She doubted Sheena could afford the pan, even if it was a wonderful item and a space saver.

"So tell me about yourself, Sheena. You said you want to design and make jewelry. Like the snood you're wearing?"

Sheena touched her head. "You guessed what it is! Most people don't know that women wore beaded headbands in ancient times. I saw some plain snoods at a Renaissance festival and knew I could make some a lot prettier. I beaded my top too. Sometimes malls have stores that sell stuff like I make. I just need to break into the market."

"Your work is lovely. You have a lot of talent." Sheena's skirt was made of overlapping layers of diaphanous scarves. The tunic top had lots of beads and fringe sown on. Kate thought she just might find her niche market. "I can see your designs in stores. What about personal dreams? Do you want a family?"

"Yeah. A big family. I want six kids. Three girls and three boys." She laughed. "But I'll take whatever I get. I love kids. Tom thinks Copper Mill is the perfect place to raise a family." Her smile faded. "I don't know. I miss the city. There's so much more to do. He says it's not so expensive here, so we can afford to get our own place someday." Her long curls bounced when she gave her head a little toss. "Not yet, but when he gets his business started. I want a house and a yard with a white fence—you know, the whole cottage-in-the-country thing like in the magazines. I want to grow roses and have apple trees and a rope swing."

"Sounds idyllic."

They'd just finished the last dish when the door from the garage opened and the men came into the house talking and laughing amicably. They sat at the kitchen table and laid the garage diagram on the tabletop.

"Are you men ready for dessert?" Kate asked.

"You bet," Paul said. He turned to Tom. "You're in for a treat."

"If it's anything like those chocolate-chip cookies you brought over, I can't wait. Those were great," Tom said. He looked down to study the diagram.

"Thank you, Tom." Kate took small plates out of the cupboard and carried them to the table, along with a golden pecan pie. "Would you like some coffee?" she asked.

Tom looked up. "Yes, please."

"I'll pour it," Sheena said, taking cups out of the cupboard.

Kate was impressed. In the few minutes they'd been working in the kitchen, Sheena had figured her way around. She was efficient and eager to please, as well as artistic. A good combination for a businesswoman.

As the women took their places at the table, the men were still discussing materials for Paul's garage project.

"Have you figured out what you want?" Kate asked.

"Tom made sense out of my ideas and sketched a plan. He's going to take on the project for me. We'll hit the hardware store tomorrow and buy materials."

"That's wonderful," Kate said, beaming.

She knew Paul was very talented, but construction had never been one of his interests. He loved projects and entered into each new endeavor with enthusiasm. Paul was thorough and tenacious, always finishing what he started, but in this case, she knew there would be frustration ahead.

It seemed like the Lord had placed Tom and Sheena in their pathway. She didn't know what God had in mind, but she was open to his leading. With Tom helping build the garage work area, Paul would have many opportunities to encourage the young man.

KATE ANTICIPATED A BREAKTHROUGH Wednesday morning as she headed to the library. She'd wanted to get back there the day before, but things had come up.

Two inches of snow had fallen overnight. The trees were flocked and pine branches bowed gracefully under their white frosting. Kate loved the muted sounds and softened morning light. The town seemed to be slumbering late that morning. Livvy was busy cataloging a new shipment of books when she walked in. Kate made her way upstairs. She considered looking through the history books, but she needed current information, not history, so she started another Internet search instead.

She resumed where she'd left off, typing "commemorative copper mining medallion" into the search engine. As before, thousands of sites came up, with references to numismatics and exonumismatics. Kate had learned that there was a difference between collectors of coins of legal tender and those who collected commemorative coins, medals, and tokens, which helped narrow her options. The Copper Mill coin fell into the category of exonumia.

Further limiting her search, she typed in "the Old Copper Road," which appeared on the coin and had historical significance to mines in the region. She found sites concerning the road, but not the coin.

After an hour of fruitless searches, she found a keyword link to a collector of trinkets, trash, and tokens with a list of states, including Tennessee. She clicked on the link and came up with a roughly designed Web site that had photographs of railroad memorabilia, mining paraphernalia, assorted tokens, and medals for sale, and finally, a copper coin that looked like it might resemble the one from Copper Mill.

Kate's attention caught on the grainy picture. She enlarged the screen. It didn't help. The image just blurred. There was a note for serious inquiries only and an e-mail address.

Kate clicked on the link and shot off a list of questions about the coin, asking for a clearer picture, for details of the coin's inscriptions, and the price, saying she was interested in mining memorabilia.

She signed her first name and gave her e-mail address. If Skip was the seller, he wouldn't reply, but she didn't believe he'd taken the coin. She wrote down the Web site and e-mail address. There was no phone number or indication where it came from, so she asked where she could see the coin in person, then hit Send.

Hoping she'd get an answer soon, Kate checked her e-mail and sent off a few messages to her family and friends in San Antonio. When she finished, she checked her in-box one more time. No response had arrived from the vendor.

Reluctantly, she logged off. Her dial-up e-mail connection at home was slow, but she could use it to check for a reply later.

It was eleven thirty when Kate went down the library stairs. Livvy was behind the front horseshoe-shaped counter. She looked up over the top of her reading glasses and saw Kate, then glanced at her watch. "Got time for a quick lunch?" Livvy asked.

"I do. Then I can tell you what I just found."

"Now you've got me curious. Let me grab my coat."

Kate waited till Livvy returned, bundled up against the chilly day. The sun had burned away the thin haze and sparkled off the snow like thousands of dancing crystals. Kate's skin tingled, and her breath puffed out in little clouds as they walked the short distance to the Country Diner.

As soon as they seated themselves at a booth, LuAnne Matthews came to the table.

"I was hoping you'd come in today." She tucked her pencil behind her ear. "Have you figured out who stole that coin yet?"

Kate shook her head, glancing around to see if anyone was eavesdropping. LuAnne's voice was loud enough for everyone in the restaurant to hear. Luckily, the nearest customers were halfway across the room and engaged in their own conversation.

"No, but I have a few ideas."

LuAnne leaned closer. "Good. I hope you find the burglar soon. Things keep pilin' up against poor Skip."

"I've heard the rumors going around," Kate said, not wanting to perpetuate more gossip.

"This isn't rumor. I heard this from Gertie herself."

Kate's ears pricked up. "You've talked to Gertie? Did she see something?"

Livvy leaned closer to LuAnne to hear better.

"Not really," LuAnne said. "She didn't see Skip or anyone take the coin, but next best thing. She said she got the key from Skip two days before the crime so she could clean the inside of the glass. She does that monthly whether it needs it or not, she said. And Skip came out to watch her, like he didn't have anything better to do than stand around and ask her questions."

"That doesn't prove anything," Livvy said.

LuAnne blushed, her face turning just a few shades lighter than her bright red hair. "She said he waited until she was done. When she handed the key back to him, he took out a neckerchief and rubbed that key until it shone. It's brass, you know. And he kept staring at the coin. He was still staring at it when she walked away. She feels guilty that she might have given him the idea to steal it."

"Why would she think that?"

LuAnne shrugged. "Beats me."

The door opened, and several people came in. LuAnne looked toward the door. "I gotta get back to work." She took an order book out of her apron pocket. "What can I get y'all?"

"I'll take the soup of the day and cheese biscuits," Livvy said.

"Sounds good. Make that two." Kate watched LuAnne walk away, then turned back toward Livvy. "What do you know about Gertie Crowe?"

Livvy was frowning. "Not a lot. She keeps to herself. She moved here when her daughter was little and worked in the school cafeteria. About ten years ago, she started cleaning businesses and government buildings. Her daughter's grown now and has a young son. She came into the library about a month ago."

"What's her daughter's name?"

"Prissy—short for Priscilla, I think. I talked to her a bit. Seems she's getting a divorce and moved back in with her mother. The boy is a whirlwind," Livvy said, shaking her head. "We had to corral him at the library. He was intent on removing all the books from the shelves."

Kate nodded. "Arlene mentioned her. Prissy joined her exercise class at Town Hall and brought her son with her."

"I don't think Prissy works, which must put a strain on Gertie. I see her occasionally at the Mercantile. She always looks tired, but that's nothing new. She works hard. I tried befriending her years ago, but she never accepted any of my invitations."

"*Hmm.* I tried to talk to her yesterday at Town Hall. She clearly didn't want to talk to me. I suppose she could have been too busy. If the daughter is at home, she isn't answering the phone, and Gertie hasn't returned my phone calls."

Livvy shrugged. "As far as I know, Gertie doesn't have any close friends. She just works and goes home. I feel sorry for her, but I guess she wants to be left alone."

LuAnne brought their food. The restaurant was filling up, so she left their lunches and hurried to another table.

Kate stared at her steamy soup, thinking about Gertie and Prissy as she stirred it.

"Do you think Gertie's involved in the coin's disappearance?" Livvy asked.

Kate stopped stirring and looked up. "I don't know. It's possible."

"But the evidence seems stacked against Skip."

"What evidence? As far as I know, the case against Skip is strictly circumstantial. Like you told LuAnne. Gertie's observations don't prove anything."

Livvy let out a short laugh. "I guess I did, but it doesn't look good. The boys asked around, and there's no talk of anyone pulling a prank by removing the coin. Someone would be bragging by now, so my idea of it being a prank doesn't sound plausible."

"No, it doesn't." Kate glanced around again. Everyone was talking and laughing, so she doubted she'd be heard. "I found a coin on the Internet that looks a lot like Copper Mill's coin. I couldn't be certain. I sent an e-mail to the seller. Now I just have to wait for a reply."

"Wow. What if it really is our coin?"

"If it is, I may not hear back."

"Not if it's someone who knows you and your e-mail address."

"True." *And that could mean Skip*, Kate thought. From Livvy's serious gaze, Kate knew she was thinking the same thing.

"Who has a key to Town Hall besides the mayor and Skip? Someone with a key could have gone in Wednesday night or Thursday morning," Livvy said.

"The town council members, the cleaning lady, and the sheriff all have keys, but anyone wanting to use the multipurpose room can get a key to Town Hall. The display-case key is kept on a hook in the deputy's office, which is open, even when the deputies are out on patrol. Even I could get a duplicate if I wanted to."

Livvy laughed. "I guess that makes us suspects along with everyone else in town."

"Not everyone, but the list is growing," Kate said.

Chapter Thirteen

Kate drove to the Bixby house Temporary Shelter at 1:20 PM, even though it was next door to her own house. She had a trunk full of food for the Faith Freezer Program.

She backed up to the garage and opened her trunk. Renee Lambert came out in a bright pink velour sweat suit to help her carry in the food she'd made plus several sacks of day-old breads, meats, and slightly over-ripened produce Sam Gorman had donated.

"Have you found Skip and the coin yet?" Renee wanted to know. The scent of Estée Lauder's Youth-Dew perfumed the air as she leaned over to take a casserole out of the trunk. Her little dog Kisses was under her arm.

Kate didn't want to spend the afternoon talking about the disappearance of the coin or Skip.

"No." She glanced at her watch and changed the subject. "I'm expecting Old Man Parsons' niece to meet me here. Has she come yet?"

"I haven't seen any strangers, and I've been here since noon. I heard he had company. Is she with the group staying at the Hamilton?"

"Yes. They're touring mines and museums in the area."

"What an odd thing to do in this weather," Renee said. "Maybe they have an ulterior motive, like our coin?" Renee narrowed her eyes as she watched Kate for a reaction.

"I'm sure the snow has hampered their excursions. Coming from up north, they expected it to be warmer here."

"It usually is. I wouldn't mind being stuck at the hotel in the snow. Such a beautiful place. I would have a spa treatment every day."

Renee had regular manicures, pedicures, and facials at the small but luxurious spa at the Hamilton Springs Hotel. "I'm sure the women would like that," Kate replied. She turned and carried her box of food into the house, leaving Renee to follow her.

Dot Bagley turned from stirring a large pot at the stove when Kate entered the kitchen. The white apron tied around her waist and white net covering her gray hair accented her plump figure.

"You're just in time," Dot said. "We need extra meals today thanks to this weather. A lot of people can't go out in the snow."

Kate set the box of groceries on the kitchen table. "I brought chicken divan. We can get eight servings from it. Sam gave us the makings for stew too."

"I'll work on that," Martha Sinclair said. She gave Kate one of her infectious smiles as she slowly shuffled over, but Kate saw her wince as she walked. The cold, damp weather must have been making her rheumatism worse, though she didn't complain.

"You've got company," Renee said behind Kate. She set the casserole on the counter.

Kate set a bunch of celery on the table and looked up.

"Hi, Eloise. Come on in." She introduced her to the ladies.

"Which one of you is the dietician?" Eloise wanted to know.

The women looked at each other quizzically.

"We're all volunteers," Kate explained.

"Oh. I thought . . . Never mind. I understand you've been delivering meals to my Uncle Joshua. I saw the macaroni and cheese with hot dogs you gave him on Friday. He can't eat all that cholesterol or so much dairy or acidic foods. He needs to be on a special diet."

"Don't you worry about your uncle," Martha said. "That was low fat. I fixed it myself, using low-fat cheese and turkey hot dogs in the recipe. The meal also included peas and carrots and applesauce. Can't get much healthier than that."

"Well, he had meat loaf on Monday. That can't be low fat."

"Actually, we used extra-lean ground beef and egg substitute in that recipe," Renee said. "We always include vegetables and fruits. We take good care of our elderly."

"But he throws away the vegetables and just eats the meat and dessert," Eloise responded.

From the tilt of Renee's chin, Kate could see she was ready to do battle.

"Come into the living room with me, Eloise. I'm sure we can make some adjustments for your uncle's special dietary needs."

Kate hoped they could. They merely did this as a service to elderly and shut-ins in town. None of them were professional cooks, and most of the locals preferred the rich fried Southern cooking to the lower-fat recipes. Kate had to watch that for Paul, who'd grown up nearby and loved deep-fried foods.

Eloise sat in a chair across from Kate and opened her large handbag. She took out several folded pieces of paper. "Uncle Joshua has high cholesterol and rheumatism. Here's his diet." She handed it to Kate.

Kate looked at the top page. It called for no salt, no MSG, low-acidic foods, and high potassium. It gave a short list of allowed foods. Some of it they could accommodate, but she couldn't imagine him eating figs and nuts or taking vinegar. Other pages talked about cleansing diets and exercise.

Eloise went into detail about eliminating coffee, sweets, white flour, and meat, especially pork. "I bought fish-oil capsules and vitamin C for him. Please make sure he takes them every day."

Kate knew Joshua loved his coffee and sweets. She suspected they'd have a fight on their hands if they tried to make him take vitamin supplements.

"Are these instructions from his doctor?" Kate asked.

"No, but they're from a specialist in the field. I found the diet on the Internet."

"We'll see what we can do," Kate said, careful not to promise anything. She stood. "If his doctor prescribes a diet, he might be more likely to follow it."

"I've tried to get an appointment with his doctor. Until then, please prepare his meals according to this."

"I know you're concerned about your uncle and his health. We'll do what we can, but we rely on donated food and volunteers, so I can't promise anything."

Eloise sighed. "I guess that's the best I can expect. If I

could, I'd move him into my home, but he refuses to budge, and I can't move here to take care of him."

"It's difficult trying to care for our elderly loved ones, isn't it? But don't worry. Joshua is pretty healthy for his age, and he has lots of friends here who look in on him regularly."

"I do worry. That's why we came to Copper Mill. It's good to know you people understand and care. Thank you."

Kate walked to the door with her. "You're welcome. Enjoy your visit with him while you can."

"I will. I'm going over to his place now. I bought some good trail mix, and I intend to supervise his dinner. I'd prepare his meals myself while we're here, but Griff insists we see as many mining sites as possible, so I don't have time. We'll be gone all day tomorrow."

Kate watched Eloise get in her SUV and drive away. From what Kate had seen, the list had a lot of healthy foods on it, but Joshua wouldn't eat most of them. If he threw vegetables away now, he'd dump the entire meal, and that certainly wouldn't help him. She shook her head as she returned to the kitchen to help. She'd visit the old man soon to see how he was doing, but not that afternoon while Eloise was there supervising.

PAUL FOLLOWED TOM through the aisles at the Builder's Hardware on the south end of Copper Mill along the railroad tracks. Paul had been there before when he'd bought a garden hose, sprinklers, and lawn fertilizer. He'd been in the lawn-and-garden section but hadn't looked at the construction supplies. They had lumber, rebar, pipe, plumbing fixtures, wire and electrical supplies, tools, ladders—everything they would need to complete his small project or build a house.

As the men looked around, Tom jotted prices on his notepad. They stopped in front of shelving components.

"You can have steel, or we can construct a wood frame and shelves. You could also get cabinets," Tom said, pointing out several options. "Depends on what you want to spend. The cabinets give you a finished look. Shelves are versatile and less expensive."

"I'm looking for utility, not appearance. Let's keep it simple. I like the wood shelves," Paul said as they stood in front of several assembled shelves. "The wood looks sturdy, and I can get clear plastic bins to keep small items neat and tidy."

"I can make a wood frame and shelving plenty sturdy. You don't want your worktable to wobble. If we buy the lumber and assemble it ourselves, that'd save money."

"Good. Let's go with that, then."

They reached the electrical aisle. "We talked about upgrading the electrical out there. You only have one plug, so you need more outlets." He reached into a bin and pulled out several plugs. "You need three-prong plugs. We'll change out the old one and add two more." He wandered down the aisle, studying bins of fixtures. "Here." He reached into another bin. "We'll put in a GFI breaker as a safety feature. You might not need it, but better safe, you know."

Listening to Tom, Paul was getting an education. The young man knew his stuff. "Maybe we should install one of those in Kate's studio too. She uses power tools and a soldering iron on her stained-glass work."

Tom selected a second outlet and added it to the cart. They ended at the order desk where Tom supplied a list of lumber and shelving materials.

While they waited, Paul noticed a display nearby. Large shoe boxes were stacked in a pyramid, with a pair of work boots on top. They looked like good leather, and the sign said they were steel-toed. He couldn't believe the price. He went over for a closer look. He could use a good sturdy boot, especially with the winter weather they'd been having. He picked out a box his size and added it to his pile. It was a bargain he couldn't pass up.

Paul recognized several people in the store and introduced Tom around. After he paid for his purchases, he backed the truck up to the loading area, where Tom waited to make sure they got everything he'd bought, then the two drove back to the parsonage.

Paul experienced a sense of satisfaction and anticipation as he and Tom off-loaded the project materials in the side of the garage where he normally parked his pickup. The truck would have to stay outside until the project was completed. According to Tom, that would take a couple of days. By the weekend, if all went well, Paul could start using his work space.

Kate often created gifts for their children, and Paul wanted to make something for their grandchildren. He'd seen animal puzzle kits and wooden toys in the project magazine. They looked simple enough. With a jigsaw and sander, he'd whip them out in no time.

He was pretty sure he'd seen those tools in the same box where he kept his father's collector coins. Paul decided that after dinner he'd get out the boxes that had belonged to his father. Just the thought filled him with anticipation. The boxes had been packed away for years. It would be like Christmas going through them.

Tom set the last length of maple on the floor and straightened up.

"How about a cup of coffee?" Paul offered.

"Sure." Tom slapped at his pant legs, dusting off the bits of wood that had stuck to his jeans. He stomped his feet on the concrete to knock off any dirt. Paul led him inside through the garage door.

"Kate, we're back," he called out.

Kate appeared at the door to her studio. She smiled at them. "Hi, Tom. Hi, honey. I started a fresh pot of coffee when I heard you pull up. There are cookies too. Help yourself. I need to finish what I'm working on before I quit for the day."

"All right. Thanks."

Paul went into the kitchen, poured two cups of coffee, and carried them to the table. The cookies were already set out. *Bless Kate. That woman is a treasure.*

Tom plopped down and took a cookie. He ate it in two bites and washed it down with coffee.

"Your wife makes great cookies," he mumbled.

"She'll be pleased you like them," Paul said. "How's the job hunt going?"

He shrugged. "Not good. Besides the work I'm doing for you, I've got no leads."

"Did you talk to Doug Campbell?"

"Haven't had time."

"All right." He'd given Tom the information about Campbell Construction the night before. Since he'd been helping Paul, perhaps he really hadn't had time. "Have you sent out résumés?"

"Naw. I prefer to talk to people, tell 'em what I can do. I never used a résumé."

"It does help, though." Paul took a sip of coffee, then set his cup down. "It gives businesses something to look at before you talk to them. Even bidding on individual jobs, people like to see what you've done. I'd be happy to help you put one together."

"I don't know, man. I don't have great job references."

"You must have some. And you have experience. You knew exactly what to order for my project. How did you learn that? That's part of your experience."

"I worked for my dad and his friends a lot."

"You're fortunate that your father could pass on his trade to you."

"Not really." He looked at Paul as if calculating his words, then he looked away. "He spent more time ragging on me about religion than teaching me carpentry. All his guys were real religious. I mean, I believe in God and all, but not like him. He's real strict, you know. An eye for an eye and all that. He didn't like it that I quit going to church, but it's just not my thing. No offense."

"No offense taken. Not all churches are like that, you know."

Paul had met others who'd been turned off by morose, overly pious religion. He experienced joy in church but knew Tom wouldn't believe it unless he experienced it himself.

Tom nodded. "I worked with my dad a couple of summers, but he'd get impatient—he had a temper—so I quit and went out on my own. Wasn't much better. I hope it's different out here in the country."

He popped another cookie in his mouth. He followed it with a swig of coffee, then drummed his fingers against the mug. He watched his fingers, looked across the room, out the window, anywhere but directly at Paul.

"First job, the boss cheated everyone. He wanted me to cut corners, use half the screws—that sort of thing. I wouldn't do it, so he fired me. Then I worked for a guy who went broke. One week, he couldn't pay me, so I left. Next job, the boss wanted me to work fifteen hours a day, then he wouldn't pay overtime. I threatened to sue him, but he laughed. Said I wasn't union, so he didn't have to pay me."

Tom's mouth curled down in a look of distaste. "Last boss just didn't like me. He did everything he could to make my life miserable. I couldn't take it. That's when I told Sheena we were moving."

"What about homeowners you worked for? Could you get references?"

Tom shook his head. "I just need a break. I need a chance to prove myself."

Paul didn't know what to say. According to Tom, everything was someone else's fault. Paul doubted that was entirely true.

"What if you just make a simple list of all the jobs you've done? If you take the time to do that, we can turn that list into a résumé."

"Sure." Tom looked down at the cup in his hand, swirling the coffee and staring at it as if it was something fascinating. Finally he looked up at Paul. "I was wondering . . . I mean, I'm kind of short right now. Could I have an advance on the job?"

Paul ran his hands through his salt-and-pepper hair. He didn't see a problem with offering an advance; the young man had already helped quite a bit with the project.

"Certainly." Paul pushed away from the table and stood. "I'll be right back."

He went into his office and turned on his computer. As it booted up, he opened a desk drawer and took out an envelope of cash earmarked for his workbench. He withdrew one hundred dollars, then he printed out a spreadsheet where he'd entered the project's estimated costs, including Tom's requested hourly rate and estimated time frame.

He returned to the kitchen table and sat down. At the bottom of the spreadsheet, he wrote the date and made a notation of the one-hundred-dollar payment.

"I put this together as the estimate for the project," Paul said, giving Tom the paper. "Would you look it over and make sure I've got everything down? Then if you'd sign that I've made a payment, that way I can keep track." He handed Tom the cash and a pen.

Tom picked up the five twenty-dollar bills, counted them, folded them in half, and put them in his pocket. He glanced over the figures on the page. "Looks all right, except I hate to lock in the hours. You never know what's going to come up, you know?"

"Do you foresee any problems?"

"No."

"This is just an estimate. I like to keep a record," Paul said.

"Fair enough." Tom scrawled his initials next to the payment, then gulped down the rest of his coffee and stood.

"I'd better get going. Got an important appointment to keep."

He took two more cookies and put them in his jacket pocket. "See you," he said. Then he left.

Chapter Fourteen

Thursday afternoon, Kate put her laptop computer in the car and went to the Bixby house to collect and deliver meals. The meals looked wonderful. Lightly breaded baked chicken, rice pilaf, fresh-steamed carrots and broccoli, fresh yeast rolls, and a dish of apple crisp with an oatmeal topping. That qualified as healthy, she thought.

She made her rounds, saving Old Man Parsons for last. When she parked in front of his house, his niece's big SUV was nowhere to be seen.

Kate made her way up to the front porch. The siding needed a fresh coat of paint, and the wicker chair on the porch had seen better days, but the yard and house were neat and clean. She pushed the buzzer and heard a discordant *bbrrrr*-ing somewhere inside the house. She waited a few moments and started to ring again when she heard shuffling steps, then the door opened. Old Man Parsons peered out from beneath his bushy white eyebrows at her.

"Yeah? Oh, it's you." He backed up and opened the door. "Come on in, Kate. I thought you might be my niece. She's supposed to be gone today, and it's a good thing. Couldn't abide her tongue lashing for another minute."

Kate raised her eyebrows but didn't ask about his niece. "I brought you some dinner," she said, giving him a cheerful smile. She enjoyed talking to Old Man Parsons, although he could be acerbic and gruff at times.

"It better not be that health-food stuff Eloise was trying to feed me. She said she gave you people a list of what I can eat. Can you imagine that? Nobody's told me what I can or can't eat since I was a lad in knickers. Heh?" He shuffled off toward the kitchen. Kate followed him.

"How about some healthy food that tastes good?" Kate said. "After all, if it doesn't taste good, you won't eat it, will you? Then what good is it?"

"My feelings exactly." He turned to look at her. "So what you got there?"

She told him the menu as she set it on the table.

"Is the chicken fried?"

"Oven fried," she said.

"Hmmph. Fake fried. It's not the same. My Alma used to make the best fried chicken in town. Won cook-offs, she did."

"I remember you telling me about her famous fudge pie," Kate said.

"Yes sir, best pie in the state. Care for a cup of coffee, Kate?"

"I'd love one."

Joshua smiled. "Good. Have a seat." He indicated the round oak kitchen table. "I don't get all that much company these days, except when you people bring me dinner. That young Eli Weston always comes here last and plays a game of cribbage with me." He chuckled.

Kate thought she detected a wicked twinkle in his eyes.

"He's gettin' pretty good, but he hasn't beaten me yet."

"Do you play cribbage as well as you play euchre?" she asked, knowing he was the county champion.

"Of course," he said, giving her an affronted look that she would even question such a thing. Then the twinkle was back. "When you've played games as long as I have, you know every trick. Now that nephew of mine—'course he's not my blood relative. He's married to my niece, more's the pity, but he's the one man who can beat me. Don't be spreadin' that around, though."

"I wouldn't think of it," Kate said, enjoying herself.

Joshua nodded. "I know or I wouldn't be tellin' you. A body can't be too careful. There's a heap of gossipy people around town. But not you."

"Thank you, Joshua. I take that as a compliment."

"And right you should. Now that niece of mine, she's a troublemaker. Comes in here bossin' me around. Brought me a bunch of pills, as if they're going to help me live longer. What's she think I'm doing? Ninety-three and goin' strong. Why I've eaten fried chicken, ribs, grits, and fried okra all my life, and it hasn't harmed a hair on my head."

He scratched his head and grinned. "Okay, I guess my hair's thinned out a bit, but I still got some, and I got all my marbles, if you get my drift."

"You have at that." She glanced over and noticed a matchbook on the table. *Red and yellow.* She turned her head slightly to read the logo. Her eyes grew wide. It advertised a truck stop. The same truck stop chain that was on the car wash token.

Old Man Parsons didn't smoke as far as she knew. *Did the matchbook belong to his nephew? It must. Did he take the coin?*

Or perhaps his wife or someone in their party. Kate looked away from the matchbook and smiled at Joshua. "So tell me about your niece and nephew. I know she's concerned about you."

"If she had her way, she'd be movin' me to Connecticut. Thank the good Lord, her husband has more sense. Now I could sit and jaw with him for hours. Appreciates a good story—not like Eloise. She doesn't listen. She wants to tell me what's what, but that Griff, he's a man after my own heart. Hard worker too. Worked his way through college as a lineman for the electric company. Now he's a history professor at a fancy university." He grinned. "Gets his inside knowledge from me. I've been tellin' him about the copper mines and the Old Copper Road. I was a miner back in the thirties, you know."

Kate perked up. "Yes, I know. Did you happen to get one of the commemorative coins from the mine like the one in Town Hall? I've heard there were about thirty of them made for the workers."

Old Man Parsons shook his head. "Those were for the rich folks." Then his eyes twinkled. "I've seen one, though. When I was a lad, Old Man Cline had one. He was real proud of it. He let me hold it once, but he had his eye on it the whole time."

"Did he?" Kate chuckled at Joshua's pleasure in his tale and his mention of "Old Man" Cline, since Joshua held the distinction of "Old Man" Parsons as he was now the oldest man in Copper Mill.

"Right proud he was of that coin. Near killed him to sell it when the Depression hit. Told me once it came down to the coin or the house, and the coin wouldn't keep his family warm and dry. He put a lot of stock in that coin, though. I remember Georgia and Evelyn took it pretty hard, 'cause their granddad made such a big deal about it."

Kate nodded. "I guess it's quite a prize."

"That's what my nephew says. He collects old coins and such, and he's particularly interested in the Old Copper Road and the copper mining. He teaches history, you know? I guess I already told you that."

Joshua was beginning to repeat himself, but Kate suspected it was more to prolong the visit than due to lack of clarity.

"Yes. Did you hear that Copper Mill's coin is missing? Someone took it right out of the case."

"Renee Lambert told me about it when she brought my meal the other day. Shame," he said, shaking his head and frowning. "Vandals from out of town most likely. Can't imagine anyone from around here would do such a thing."

"Seems unlikely." She didn't mention Skip or her suspicions about Joshua's niece's husband. She finished her coffee and set the cup down. "I hope you enjoy your visit with your nephew. Eloise said they'll be here another week."

He grimaced. "So she said. Too long if you ask me. He can stay, but I can't abide my niece much longer. Neither can he, truth to tell. She's always tellin' him what to do. Poor man had to sneak around to smoke his pipe. We sent her on an errand, and he was happy as a coon in a hen house, sittin' here playing checkers whilst he smoked and I talked."

He wagged his finger at Kate. "Don't you listen to her about my eating habits."

"I won't." Kate heard a car park and a door slam. She stood. "I'd better get going. I have errands to run."

"You just want to leave before my niece gets back. Can't say as I blame you." He started to rise.

"Don't get up. I'll let myself out. Thanks for the coffee and the talk."

He'd given her a lot to think about. She carried her cup to the sink, then headed for the door. Sure enough, Eloise and her husband and three of their group were coming up the steps as she went out.

"Oh. Hello Kate. Did you bring Uncle Joshua's dinner?" Eloise asked.

"Yes." She reached out to Griff and shook his hand. "I'm Kate Hanlon," she said, smiling. "I saw you at Town Hall last week. I hope you're enjoying your visit."

"Very much, thanks," he said. "You've got a nice town here, and Joshua's a fount of historical information."

"Yes he is, isn't he?"

Kate was surprised by the man's friendly manner, since he'd ignored her and even seemed like he was hiding something outside the pharmacy.

She greeted the others, then said good-bye and walked down the steps to her car, thinking about all Joshua had said, like the fact that Griff had to sneak around with his pipe smoking. That answered for his guilty appearance outside the pharmacy. He'd been hiding from his wife. Still, Kate didn't rule him out as a suspect. He'd certainly been to a truck stop and picked up the matches. Had he picked up a car wash token from the same place? The token that had been left in place of the copper coin?

According to Old Man Parsons, Griff was very interested

in the coin. Interested enough to steal it? Or had Georgia and Evelyn Cline wanted the coin badly enough to have taken it?

KATE STOPPED BY TOWN HALL on her way to the library after leaving Old Man Parsons' house. The sheriff was there, and she brought him up to date on what she'd learned about the coin's value, Griff Henley's interest, and the Cline sisters' grandfather having owned one of the coins. None of her information gave conclusive evidence, but at least it opened other options to investigate.

By the time she got to the library, school was out for the day, and the building was buzzing with teens and moms with younger children. Every computer was tied up, so Kate was glad she'd brought her own. Normally she just used the library computers, but this time she wanted to download the correspondence onto her laptop, so she could open the large files later.

She found an empty spot at a table, took out her laptop, and turned it on. It took a few moments for it to boot up, then find the library's wireless network. Once there, she downloaded her e-mail.

As an e-mail from Jjohns appeared, Kate nearly jumped out of her seat.

Dear PWKatie. From the instructions in the forum and downloading the manual, I was able to fix my truck window. I'm no expert, though, so I can't be much help. If that's your problem, I suggest you print out the door panel section of the manual for your truck.

—Jjohns

Kate quickly hit Reply.

Dear Jjohns, I saw your dialogue with Coppercop, and I'm guessing and hoping you are Jayme Johnson who's been in contact with him. I think Coppercop is Skip Spencer. He's a deputy in our town, and he's missing. We found your name among his things, along with the vehicle parts Web site address. He's a friend of mine, and it's urgent that we find him. If you have had contact with him, please let me know, and ask him to get in touch with the sheriff in Harrington County, TN. If you have any information to help us find him, we'd be very grateful.

Kate signed her full name and gave her phone number. She prayed this would lead her to Skip as she hit Send. Then she clicked to preview a large e-mail with an attachment.

It began "Dear Kate. Thank you for your interest in my old coin." She opened the e-mail and read the contents.

I've attached close-up pictures of the coin front and back. As you can see, my coin is in mint condition. It's a commemorative coin dated 1857, made of one troy ounce of .9999 pure gold overlaid with copper. I am asking $12,000.00 to be transferred electronically to my account or paid in certified U.S. funds. This is a valuable medallion, as very few were made. I live in northern Florida. If you are interested, you can come here to purchase the coin, or I can arrange delivery upon receipt of your funds. Let me know if you wish to proceed.

Northern Florida? Skip supposedly went to Florida. She couldn't believe he would answer her e-mail. Surely he would know it was from her. She'd signed it from Kate. *Does he know someone in Florida who'd fence the coin for him?*

What was she thinking? Here she was letting the sheriff and the local gossip influence her convictions.

Kate opened the first picture. Two huge photographs filled her entire computer screen. The closer she looked, the more excited she became. She went to the local history books and found the one with the facsimile of the article on the mine celebration. The original article was mounted in the display case next to where the coin had been mounted. As far as she could tell, the coin in the e-mail appeared to be identical to the Copper Mill coin.

Had she finally found the missing coin or a duplicate? Now she had to trace the seller. She would have to turn the information over to the sheriff, but she had more to learn before she did so. She didn't want to implicate an innocent party. After all, thirty coins had been made. This could be any one of them.

Kate carefully worded her reply, asking if the seller could provide proof of the coin's composition, rarity, and value. Then she asked if she could come see the coin in person. Praying she would get an answer that would lead to the thief, Kate clicked Send and watched her e-mail disappear into cyberspace.

Please, Lord, don't let it be Skip, she silently pleaded.

Chapter Fifteen

When Kate returned home, she found a message from Dolores Spencer on the telephone. Putting a kettle of water on to heat, she called Dolores back.

"Kate, the sheriff was here again asking if I've heard from Skip." Dolores was silent for a moment before she continued. "He was real nice about it, but he said I need to tell him if I've heard from Skip and I shouldn't try to protect him, 'cause I could get into trouble, and Skip wouldn't want that. H-he showed me a warrant for . . ."

Dolores' voice broke. Kate could hear her take a ragged breath.

"He's going to arrest my son for robbery. He said Skip withdrew all his savings and left town, and you saw him go."

"What I saw doesn't prove anything, Dolores. But he's right that Skip wouldn't want to involve you in his problems." *Surely Skip wouldn't risk ruining his life, even if the coin was worth ten times as much*, Kate thought. "So I'm guessing you still haven't heard from Skip?"

"No. Nothing."

"I wish I could give you some good news, but I don't have any answers yet. Right now prayer is the one thing you can do without ceasing. Paul and I are praying for Skip too, and for the real thief to be caught."

"That means a lot to me. Thank you. Please call me if you hear anything."

"I will. Now try to get some rest, and don't worry."

"All right. I'll try."

Kate heard a sniffle just before Dolores hung up. *Easier said than done*, she thought. *Could I rest and not worry if one of my children disappeared without a trace? Poor woman. How can she rest? Not easily, even with prayer. Perhaps not at all.*

To make matters worse, it looked as if the sheriff intended to call Kate as a witness against Skip. In fact, everything she'd had to tell him about Skip made the deputy appear guilty, instead of innocent, as she was trying to prove.

Lord, give Dolores your peace that passes all understanding. Only in you, Lord, can she let go and find the rest she needs. Please keep Skip safe, and somehow let Dolores know he's all right. And help me find the real thief. Thank you, Lord. Amen.

PAUL SAVED THE DOCUMENT he'd been composing on his computer and shut down. He spent a few minutes enjoying the silence of his church office and mulling over the Scripture passages he'd read, preparing for a new series of sermons.

He closed his Bible and spent a few moments in prayer, seeking the Lord's guidance and revelation. It amazed and awed him that the Bible was new and fresh every day, even after forty years in the ministry. God still revealed new truths through his Word.

Paul glanced at his watch. He needed to get home. He wanted to be there when Tom started on his workbench. Kate was there, but Paul didn't expect her to oversee his project. Since Millie Lovelace, the church secretary, had left for the day, Paul gathered his coat and locked up as he left.

Gray winter clouds had gathered, obscuring the brilliant blue sky and bright sunlight that had greeted the day. Paul had been tempted to walk to work that morning, even though the temperature barely topped freezing, but he'd had house calls to make, so he'd driven to the church. As icy rain pelted his face, he was glad to climb into the cab of his old truck.

In the short distance between the church and the parsonage, the rain turned to big fat flakes of snow. When he reached the house, he noticed that Tom's van wasn't there yet.

Leaving his truck in the driveway, Paul hurried inside. Kate had a lively fire dancing in the fireplace. She was sitting in her favorite rocking chair, reading a book. She looked up when he entered. He shook the snow off his coat and hung it on the coat tree in the entryway.

"It's snowing," he said, going over to give her a kiss. She stood and put her hands on his face.

"*Brrr.* You're freezing. Sit down by the fire. I'll get you a cup of coffee."

He went over and rubbed his hands in front of the fire. "Have you heard from Tom?"

"No. What time was he supposed to come over?" she called from the kitchen.

"I thought he'd be here by four. It's nearly four thirty."

Kate handed him a cup of coffee. He held it with both hands, letting the warmth seep in and the rich aroma fill his senses. Standing with his back to the fireplace, he looked out the window.

"The snow is beginning to stick."

Kate sidled up next to him and put her arm around his waist.

"What a pretty picture," she said. "I hope we get enough to blanket the ground so it doesn't melt off right away."

"Looks like we might."

"Maybe he's not here because of this weather. You should give him a call."

Paul nodded and walked into the kitchen. A few minutes later, he came back to the living room.

"No answer. I hope he's okay."

"I'm sure he's fine. Something must have come up."

"I suppose you're right," Paul said. But that didn't ease his disappointment.

Everything was ready. If he hadn't hired Tom, he would roll up his sleeves and start by himself. Tom had the plan and most of the tools, though. *Patience*, he told himself.

He'd planned to spend the evening working in the garage. He'd already unpacked the clamps and a hammer and screwdrivers from one box of his father's tools, then put the rest back. No sense taking them out until he had room to store them.

Kate went to get dinner on the table. He got up and helped, but he wasn't very hungry. His disappointment about Tom's no-show sapped his enthusiasm.

Now he had the evening ahead of him with nothing to do. He could start the book that he'd been meaning to read for two weeks. Somehow, that didn't seem very appealing. Not when he'd had other plans. Maybe his sermon the previous Sunday had been meant for him. *Patience*.

THE COLD HIT KATE as soon as she slipped out from beneath the covers Friday morning. She glanced out the window as she pulled on her robe. It was still dark outside, but she could make out the white layer of snow clinging to the bare maple branches and the ground. The sight buoyed her spirits.

She knew that eventually the snow would stop and the clouds would lift, unveiling beautiful white-draped mountain peaks. Kate loved the seasonal changes that were so much more dramatic than they'd been in Texas.

She made coffee and started a fire in the fireplace, then she took her Bible and coffee to her favorite rocking chair, where she could enjoy the cheery flames and look at the evidence of winter outside the sliding-glass doors.

Skip was on her mind that morning, just as he had been every morning since he disappeared. She wondered where he'd gone and if he was safe or in some kind of trouble. He certainly had trouble enough here in Copper Mill. How could life get turned upside down so quickly?

Opening her Bible, she turned to the Psalms, which always brought her comfort. She found Psalm 121, a favorite. As she read out loud, she turned the psalm into a prayer for Skip.

> Psalm 121. *A song of ascents.*
> I lift up my eyes to the hills—
> where does my help come from?
> My help comes from the Lord,
> the Maker of heaven and earth.

Father, please don't let Skip's foot slip. Watch over him and be his shade by day and his shelter in the night. Keep him from harm. If he is in trouble, rescue him. Bring him back safely, and bring the truth to light. If he's falsely accused, exonerate him. You know I want to help him, Lord. Show me how.

She went on silently, praying for Dolores and for the sheriff, for Tom and Sheena, for Wendy and Billy, for each of her children and grandchildren, and for Paul.

When she finally said "Amen" and lifted her head, Paul came out of the kitchen with a cup of coffee. His smile and sleep-ruffled hair filled her heart with gratitude.

"Good morning," she said, smiling from her soul. How precious it was to share such intimate moments with her heavenly Father.

"Morning." Paul kissed the top of her head. "Are you ready for a refill?"

"Actually, I was thinking about starting breakfast. How about some hot grits?"

"It's the right weather for it. With walnuts and dried cranberries?"

"Coming right up."

As she went into the kitchen, the telephone rang. She started to reach for the phone, but it stopped ringing. She assumed that Paul picked it up in his study.

She was stirring the hot cereal when Paul entered the kitchen. "Are you planning to be home this morning?" he asked.

"I can be."

"Well, don't change your plans if you have someplace to go."

"No. I want to check for an e-mail response, but I can do that from here with our dial-up. Was that Tom?"

"It was Sheena. She apologized for last night. Said some-thing came up. Tom wants to come over this morning to start in the garage. He should get here around nine."

"I'll stay here, unless you'd rather have him wait."

"All the materials are here. I don't want to delay any longer. I'll come home at lunch to see how he's doing. You can call me if he has any problems."

"All right." She dished up two bowls of hot cereal. They usually ate grits with melted butter, salt, and pepper, but the brown sugar, dried fruit, and nuts with a little half-and-half on top made a great alternative.

"Looks great," he said, taking a bowl. He pasted on a bright smile.

They sat at the table, and Paul gave thanks for their break-fast and their day and asked a special blessing for Tom. One of the things Kate loved about Paul was his determination to have a good attitude, no matter what disappointments he faced. She knew he really wanted to be part of his project.

Kate completed her morning routine quickly, expecting Tom to arrive at any time.

At nine thirty, Kate turned on her laptop and went online. After several long minutes of waiting to connect, she went to their Internet service provider's Web site to check her e-mail.

As she'd hoped, there was a reply from the coin seller wait-ing to be downloaded. Like the day before, the file contained attachments that were large—way too big for their dial-up service to download in any reasonable amount of time. When she tried to open the message, her computer froze. She'd have to wait until she could go to the library.

She went to her studio. She'd gotten several orders for

stained-glass gifts that she needed to fill and ship for
Valentine's Day, plus some items she'd promised for Smith
Street Gifts. Though she advertised specific items and colors
on her Web site, she always had a few special orders.

She packed a tulip night-light for one customer and a but-
terfly garden stake for another. She set them aside to take to
the post office. The jiggly garden stakes were popular this year.
She had an order for three bright blue dragonflies. She got out
a sheet of robin's egg blue and white ring mottle to cut the
bodies. She worked for a while, glancing at the clock every fifteen minutes or so.

She'd listen for the doorbell or a knock on the door or a van
to pull up. She would lapse into concentration and block everything from her mind except the cut pieces of colored glass,
strips of copper foil, and her task. Then she'd jerk to attention
suddenly, glance at the clock, and listen for approaching
sounds.

Nothing. She hoped she hadn't become so absorbed in her
task that she'd missed him. But Tom's older-model van was
noisy, and the studio door was open, so she would have heard
anyone at the door.

At eleven thirty, the phone rang, jarring her to attention.
She put down her tools and hurried to the phone.

"Hello?"

"Kate. Did Tom get started all right?"

"Paul. He's not here yet. I've been working on stained
glass, but I'm sure I would have heard him."

"I'm sure you would. I wonder what's keeping him."

She heard Paul sigh.

"I have one more appointment, then I'll come home. If he

hasn't arrived by then, I'll go by his house and see if he's all right."

"Good idea."

After she hung up, Kate finished her task, then put away her stained-glass paraphernalia. It was 11:45 when she went to the kitchen to start lunch.

The day called for soup. Kate heated a copper sauté pan and added a dab of butter and olive oil while she thin-sliced a large, sweet onion. She sautéed the onion and added a dash of Worchestershire sauce and a few drops of Tabasco. When the mixture began to brown, she added two cans of concentrated beef broth, some apple cider, a bay leaf, and a pinch of thyme.

As the broth simmered, she took out a loaf of French bread to slice.

A knock on the door stopped her. She put down the knife and went to answer it.

Tom stood on the doorstep. In place of a jacket, he wore a beat-up gray sweatshirt with the hood up.

"Come in." She stood out of the way. "You look cold."

"Not too bad." He removed the hood. His hair stuck up in shaggy spikes. He raked his fingers through his hair, attempting to tame it. "Sorry I couldn't get here sooner. Sheena dropped me off on her way to work." He gave her a sheepish smile.

"I'll let you get started." Kate opened the garage door. She flipped on the light. "Paul should be home for lunch soon. Do you need anything?"

"I need to open the overhead door. I left my tools outside."

"There's the button," she said, pointing to a button on the wall next to the door. "I'll be in the kitchen if you need anything."

"Thanks. I'll be fine."

"When Paul gets home, we'd love to have you join us for lunch. I'm making soup."

He nodded but didn't reply, already looking around at the materials. Kate left him to start his workday . . . a few hours late.

Chapter Sixteen

Paul had a couple of hours free for lunch. He invited Tom to join them, promising that Kate's onion soup was worth the time. He knew Tom arrived late, but he didn't want to sacrifice getting to know the young man just to make a point. Besides, the smell of Kate's soup was so tantalizing that the poor guy would have suffered if he hadn't joined them.

Paul helped Kate assemble the bowls, and she poured the hot soup over thick slices of toasted French bread, then topped each with provolone cheese and popped the bowls under the broiler until the cheese melted. She set the steamy bowls of soup in front of the men, along with slices of apple, carrot sticks, peanut butter, and assorted crackers.

After Paul asked a blessing on their meal and their day, Tom dug into his soup. He took several spoonfuls, then looked up at Kate.

"This is great. Maybe you could give the recipe to Sheena. She's pretty good, but she only knows how to make about ten things." He had the grace to look embarrassed. "I'm not dissing her. She really tries. Her spaghetti's real good."

Kate gave him an understanding smile. "I've had almost thirty years to work on my cooking, with Paul as my guinea pig. He'll tell you, not all my experiments were successful. I'd be happy to share this recipe and any others she'd like."

When they finished, Kate offered Paul and Tom another bowl of soup. They declined, so she carried their bowls to the sink, then excused herself and headed to the library while they got back to work.

Kate didn't see Livvy when she entered the library. She went upstairs and found an empty spot to set up her laptop and connect to the library's high-speed Internet.

The message from the coin vendor took a couple of minutes to download. When it landed in her in-box, she read:

Dear Kate, I've attached a copy of the original papers that accompanied the coin. My great-great-uncle had invested in the mine. The coin is from his estate. This should satisfy you as to the coin's intrinsic value and rarity. You can call me if you have any questions. I'd be happy to have you come see the coin. It is kept in a bank safety-deposit box, so please let me know when to expect you.

The woman signed her full name and included her address in Lake City, Florida. Kate opened the attachment. As before, it was huge. She scrolled along the top, reading the heading. Superior Mint and Casting Company. Charlotte, North Carolina. The description of the coin, its composition and purity of the gold, and the limited minting were all there, including the name of the recipient: Colonel Benjamin Harding of Chattanooga, Tennessee.

That was it. Positive proof. This was not *the* coin from Town Hall, but it was an exact duplicate. It was very rare and undoubtedly worth what the seller was asking. She'd reached a dead end as far as proving Skip's innocence. Kate didn't know whether to rejoice or be disappointed.

She responded to the e-mail, thanking the woman for her correspondence and letting her know that she would not be purchasing the coin. She told the woman she was looking for an identical coin that had disappeared from their Town Hall and hers obviously was not the missing coin. Then she wished her success and blessings and sent off her reply.

THE CUT LENGTHS OF MAPLE SLATS for the workbench legs leaned against the garage's back wall. It didn't look like much, but Paul knew it represented progress. He tried to imagine the finished product. He couldn't wait. Tom might have started late, but he'd gotten down to work in the short time he'd been there.

"What can I do?" Paul asked.

"We need to assemble the sides first. The legs will be L-shaped posts. I'm using rabbet joints. See how I've cut a notch down the length of this board?" he said, holding up one length of leg where a long indentation had been cut out of one side of the wood. "I'll cut each leg piece this way, then miter them together. You can glue them."

Paul nodded, unsure what a rabbet joint was but confident he'd learn. He watched Tom use the miter saw he'd brought with him to cut the wood without even wearing goggles. He finished a cut, turned off his saw and blew the sawdust off the piece, then handed it to Paul.

"Brush it off, then glue it up along both edges of the cut," he said. "Glue's over there." He pointed to a pile of supplies.

Paul followed the directions. When he put the two boards together, fitting the edge of one into the notch on the other, he took his time making sure the ends lined up exactly.

"Not too tight," Tom said, turning from the saw. He'd shut it off, killing the screechy noise.

After working together for an hour, Paul and Tom had the legs of the bench cut and one side assembled with a piece of fiberboard.

When the garage door rose and Kate pulled in, Paul checked his watch. Time to get back to the church. He had an appointment soon. He looked down at his clothes. Fine sawdust covered his slacks and shirt.

"I've got to go, Tom. I need to spend a couple of hours at the office this afternoon."

"Sure thing. I might not be here when you get home. Depends on when Sheena comes to pick me up. If not, I'll see you first thing Monday morning."

"All right. See you then." Paul brushed some of the sawdust off his clothes, then went inside to change.

Kate was in the kitchen when he came out in clean clothes.

"I'm going back to the church," he said.

She turned around, a wooden spoon, dripping with brown batter, in her hand. "Is Tom still working?"

"Yes. He'll keep at it until Sheena comes to get him if that's all right with you. What's cooking?"

"I thought I'd try out a low-sugar cookie recipe for the Faith Freezer Program."

Paul raised an eyebrow. "Working out your puzzle, huh?"

Kate nodded. Her brows knit together in a perplexed frown. "I heard back about the coin. It was a lady in Florida who inherited it. She had the original papers for it."

"I'm sorry honey. I know you were hoping you'd found the coin. You'll discover the truth when the time is right."

She pointed the gooey spoon at him. "Just be glad I have something productive to do with these goodies. I'm likely to be baking up a storm until I figure this out."

He laughed, earning him a glower from his sweet-natured wife. Paul gave her a kiss, erasing her pouty expression. He thought at that moment that he never grew tired of her kisses. "I am. Very thankful."

KATE HAD JUST TAKEN THE LAST TRAY of her second batch of cookies out of the oven when the doorbell rang. She set the pan on the counter and went to the door. Sheena stood on the porch shivering. She wore a light cardigan sweater. The sun had peeked out for a while but then disappeared behind a bank of dark clouds.

"Come in, come in." Kate stepped aside. "Don't you have a coat?"

"Yeah, but I didn't think I'd need it. The sun was shining by the time we left the house this morning. The snow was melting."

"Tom's still working, but you're welcome to join me in the kitchen if he's not ready to leave. There are fresh cookies, and I can fix some hot cocoa."

"That sounds delicious. Thanks." Sheena went into the garage.

Kate noticed she'd left a smudge of flour on the doorknob. She wiped it off with her apron, and then went to the kitchen and washed off her hands.

She was mixing cocoa in a pan—one of her many special hot-cocoa recipes with a touch of honey and cinnamon—when Sheena came into the kitchen.

"Tom isn't finished yet. You sure you don't mind if I hang around and wait for him?"

"Not at all. I'm glad for the company." Kate took two of her nicest mugs out and filled them with the hot drink, then handed one to Sheena. "Shall we go sit by the fire in the living room?"

"Sure. These are really pretty," Sheena said. Kate picked up her mug and a plate of cookies and went into the living room.

"How was work today?"

"Good. I just worked lunch. It's kind of weird jumping around to different hours all the time, but they just call me when they're busy. They had a good crowd. Then I did some shopping." Sheena tossed her head and pushed her long ringlets over her shoulder. Her eyes sparkled. She set her mug on the lamp table next to her and clasped her hands together almost like a prayer. "I'm so excited. A couple of ladies came in today and bought two of my pins. They said I should sell them in Pine Ridge. I hope they're right."

"I hope so too. When do you want me to take you?"

"How about Tuesday? I'm off for sure then."

"Sounds great to me," Kate said.

Sheena looked around the room and raised the mug to her

lips. "I like the way you've decorated. It's real cozy here." She looked up at the mantle over the fireplace. "Is that your family?" She got up to look at the framed pictures.

Kate went over to the fireplace. "That's our son, Andrew and his wife, Rachel, then Ethan and Hannah," she said, pointing out her grandchildren. "This one is Melissa and her husband, John, holding Mia Elizabeth."

"She's adorable. I can't wait to have kids."

"And that's our daughter Rebecca standing with us in front of our house in San Antonio." The house was a white two-story colonial with dark green shutters at the windows and a wide porch and columns across the front. Large pink rhododendron bushes showed on each side of Kate and Rebecca.

"She's gorgeous. Is she a model?"

"She's an actress and singer in New York."

"Wow. That must be fun. Your house was beautiful. How come you moved here?"

Kate smiled. "The opportunity came up, and we prayed about it for a long time. When we both felt this was where God wanted us, the doors seemed to open for us to move right away. So here we are."

"Wow. Did it turn out good, or do you wish you could go back?"

"We love it here. I miss my family and our friends from our old church. Sometimes I miss the amenities of the city, but God's blessed us here many times over. We hope we're a blessing to others here too."

Sheena came to the last picture. Paul was standing proudly beside his cherished classic Lexus sports car in front of their church in San Antonio.

"Is that the church where your husband was the preacher?"

"Yes. It's called Riverbend Community Church." The church was spacious and modern. It had been very small when they first moved there, but it had grown into a very large church by the time they left.

"His car's really cool. Did you have to leave it there?"

"No. We brought it to Copper Mill."

"What happened to it?"

"Well, the church burned down the day we moved here."

Sheena's eyes widened. "Man, that's bad luck."

"It was tragic, but it turned into a blessing."

"*Ha*. I don't see how *that's* possible," Sheena said, planting her hands on her hips.

"God often turns tragedy to good. No one was hurt, and now we have a lovely new church, almost identical to the old one, and people grew closer when everyone worked together to rebuild."

"Did his car burn in the fire?"

"Oh no. He sold it to help rebuild the church."

"So now he drives an old truck, when he could be driving his beautiful sports car? That's so sad."

Kate smiled. "Paul enjoyed that car for a season. Now he enjoys the new church and all the people here who have become like our family."

Sheena shook her head. She appeared genuinely sad for Paul and completely confused. Kate just smiled at her. Perhaps someday she would understand.

Tom stuck his head inside the house from the garage. "Hey, you ready to go?" he called. "I don't want to come in the house. I'm really dirty and dusty."

Sheena grabbed her sweater and practically ran to the garage. She stopped and turned to Kate.

"Thanks for the cocoa and cookies." She gave Kate a little wave.

Kate waved back, but Sheena was already closing the door behind her.

Chapter Seventeen

Kate didn't expect to see Tom and Sheena at church, so she wasn't looking for them or anyone new. She was totally surprised when Dolores and Trixie scooted into the pew next to her. The congregation was standing, singing the first hymn.

She gave the two women a welcoming smile and handed them an open hymnal. It was a familiar old song, so she knew it by heart. Dolores gave her a grateful smile. She and Trixie found their place, and their voices joined in.

After the music, Paul gave a message on the fruit of the Spirit, speaking on patience.

"In Colossians," Paul said, "in chapter one, verses nine to twelve, the Apostle Paul tells the church that he and his companions had been praying for them, asking God to reveal his will and give them wisdom and understanding. 'And we pray this in order that you may live a life worthy of the Lord and may please him in every way: bearing fruit'—there's that fruit of the Spirit—'in every good work, growing in the knowledge of God, being strengthened with all power according to his glorious might so that you may have great endurance and patience, and joyfully giving thanks to the Father...'

"God's power gives us the strength to endure with patience and joy."

As Paul prayed that the Lord would bless the reading of his Word and would enlighten them, Kate prayed that Dolores would know beyond all doubt that God was with her through this difficult time, and he was with Skip too.

At the end of the prayer, Dolores had tears in her eyes. Kate reached over and squeezed her hand. She squeezed back but didn't look over.

The congregation stood as Sam Gorman played a postlude. Kate rose beside Dolores.

"I'm so glad you came. I've been wondering how you're doing," Kate said.

Dolores gave her a halfhearted smile. She had dark circles under her eyes. "I'm doing all right."

Kate nodded. Trixie, who was talking with Renee, turned away from them. "How long will Trixie be with you?"

"She says she's going home in a week whether Gary is ready or not. She's getting antsy, I think, but she doesn't complain. And she keeps running into people she knew, like Renee."

"That's right. I'd forgotten she used to live here." Kate smiled. "How are the repairs on the gas leak coming along?"

"She's not exactly sure. She hasn't heard from Gary in two days. She's left messages at his repair shop, but he hasn't returned her calls. She's upset with him, but mostly worried. I told her he's probably just busy." Dolores shook her head. "These boys don't realize what they put their mothers through. Just because they're adults doesn't mean we don't worry."

"True. What would we do if we didn't have prayer?" Kate said. "Sometimes that's all that keeps me going."

"Skip's never been gone like this before. Even when he's camping, at least I know what he's doing. If I just knew . . . That verse Pastor Hanlon read talks about getting strength and patience from God. I don't seem to have much of either. I certainly don't feel joyful."

Kate didn't know what to say. As she stood there looking at Dolores, she realized there was nothing she could do that would help except finding Skip and proving his innocence, and so far, she'd failed on both counts.

Dolores gave her a quick hug. "Thanks for listening and being here for me," she said. Then she turned to Trixie. "We'd better get going."

The two women stepped into the aisle and headed toward the front door. Paul was standing in the narthex, greeting parishioners as they left. Kate saw the two stop and speak to him. He had a gift for making people feel welcome and important. Hopefully Dolores had found the safe haven she needed at this moment.

KATE WAS READY TO LEAVE THE HOUSE to run errands Monday morning, keys in hand, when Tom pulled up in his van, blocking the driveway.

Since they hadn't heard from Tom earlier that morning, Paul had gone to the office at his regular time. Kate slipped the keys in her jacket pocket and hung it on the coat tree before she answered the door.

"Hi, Kate," Tom said, removing his baseball cap. He stamped his feet on the welcome mat, then crossed the threshold. "I've got a little time to work."

"Good morning. Go ahead out to the garage," she said, resigned to postponing her errands until Paul came home for lunch. At least she didn't have an appointment. "Is there anything I can get you?"

"You got any coffee?"

"I do. I'll bring you a cup."

As soon as Tom went to the garage, Kate called Paul and let him know Tom had arrived. He promised to come home for lunch. Kate hung up and took a cup of coffee to Tom.

Adjusting her schedule, she took out a dust cloth and can of polish and set to work on the furniture. She'd planned to clean house that afternoon.

Kate loved the rich luster and lemony scent of polished wood. Add pine boughs, beeswax candles, and a pot of something good bubbling on the stove, and the house would smell a little like heaven.

She heard a tap on the door from the garage, then the door opened a crack, and Tom poked his head through.

"I've got to leave. Tell Preach I'll be back sometime tomorrow."

"Do you want to call him at the office and talk to him?"

"Naw. I'll talk to him tomorrow. I'll go out through the garage. Will you close it after me?"

"Sure." Kate put down the can of polish and went to the door.

The overhead door rose, and Tom went out, carrying his bucket of tools.

He tossed the bucket in the back of his van, then climbed into the driver's seat. The engine roared to life, puffing out a plume of black smoke. Kate pushed the button to lower the the garage door.

Kate glanced at the workbench area, then looked at her watch. It had been forty-five minutes since Tom arrived. She went to the kitchen and called Paul's cell phone.

When he answered, she said, "I hate to tell you this, but Tom just left for the day."

"He's not coming back?"

"No. He said he'd see you tomorrow, but he didn't say when."

She heard Paul's sigh. "He said the job would take ten to fifteen hours. He didn't say how many weeks."

"I'm sorry, honey. And I won't be here tomorrow. I promised Sheena I'd take her to Pine Ridge."

"I'll stop by their house before I come home this evening and see if I can talk to him. I guess I won't come home for lunch."

Kate knew Paul was frustrated and disappointed, though he quickly adjusted his plans to make the most of his day. *Nothing like a little comfort food to cheer one up, and Paul wasn't the only one who could use a little cheer*, she thought, so she postponed her errands a little while longer and put on a pot of water to boil.

She took boneless, skinless chicken breasts out of the freezer and put them in the water with bay leaves to cook while she cut up onions and celery and prepared a low-fat adaptation of good ol' chicken and dumplings. Doubling her usual recipe, which she made up as she went along, Kate readied a glass casserole dish for the second batch.

An hour later, she drove to Dolores' house. She wanted to check in on Skip's mother and try to bring her some comfort.

The sun was so bright, she had to put on her sunglasses. The warmth felt wonderful after the recent cold weather.

She carried the casserole to the door and rang the bell. Dolores answered. She was dressed in a housecoat, and her hair was unkempt. She looked as if she'd just gotten out of bed. Kate could hear the television in the background, tuned to one of the daytime talk shows.

"Would you like to come in?" Dolores asked.

"No, thanks. I'm just out running errands. I made chicken and dumplings, and I have way too much for the two of us, so I thought you might like some." Kate held out the dish.

"Why, thank you." Dolores accepted the dish. She seemed surprised, as if she wasn't expecting a kindness.

"You're welcome. I was glad to see you yesterday. I know this is a hard time for you."

A thought flashed into Kate's mind. "You know, it's absolutely beautiful outside. You and Trixie ought to get out and go for a drive while the weather's so nice." The woman needed some fresh air—that much was obvious.

"Perhaps we will. I haven't wanted to go out. Poor Trixie. She went to get a few things at the store, but I'm sure she's bored. She won't want to come see me ever again."

"I'm sure she understands."

"Yes. She's a good friend. I don't know what I'd do without her right now."

They talked for a few minutes, then Kate left to complete her errands.

She stopped at the post office and went inside to buy

stamps. A young woman with a little boy stood in line in front of her. The boy was reaching over the edge of a table stacked with various forms and packaging materials. He grabbed a handful of certified-mail forms and pulled them to the floor. They went all over.

"Michael, stop it," the woman demanded. The boy ignored her and ran over to the trash can and began pulling advertising flyers out of the container. The woman didn't try to stop him.

"Prissy, how are you?" Kate heard from behind her. She turned.

"Hi, Kate," Arlene Jacobs said, giving her a bright smile. "Have you met Prissy Ranken?"

Arlene introduced them, and Kate realized she was meeting Gertie Crowe's daughter and grandson.

"Next," the teller called. Prissy moved up to the counter and presented a form to pick up held mail.

"You coming to exercise class Wednesday?" Arlene asked Prissy.

"Yeah. I have to bring Michael, unless mom will watch him. She has a cleaning job real early that morning, and she said she'd try to finish in time for the class."

The clerk came back, and Prissy turned around. She took one look at the legal-looking envelope and backed away.

"I'm not accepting that thing," she said. "It's another collection letter, and I'm not paying it. That belongs to my ex. Send it back."

The clerk shrugged, marked it refused, and tossed the letter into a bin. Prissy grabbed Michael's hand and pulled him along out the door.

"See you," she told Arlene, who watched her go with a perplexed expression.

Kate bought her stamps, then hurried to the library. She found an empty computer station and logged on to the Internet.

As messages downloaded, a message from Jjohns popped into her in-box. She opened it first.

Dear Kate. I am Jayme Johnson, and I did exchange e-mails and a couple of phone calls with Skip Spencer. I didn't know he was a deputy. We talked about our trucks. I'm restoring one like his. I'm further along, but I have a guy nearby who specializes in restoring Ford trucks. I told Skip about him. I'll call him and pass along your message, in case Skip gets in touch. I hope he's all right. He seems like a nice guy. I'd like to hear from him again too.

—Jayme

Kate was disappointed that Jayme didn't lead her to Skip or give her the name of the restorer, but she couldn't blame Jayme for not giving out names and addresses. She had no way of knowing if Kate was really a friend of Skip's. Still, Jayme's e-mail had revealed a couple of snippets. Enough to pick up his trail, Kate hoped.

Kate mentally evaluated her new information as she drove home. Jayme hadn't said, but Kate decided to go on the premise that she lived in Florida. She would map out what she knew to find Skip.

Prissy Ranken was another new element. She had financial problems. She'd been at Town Hall on Wednesday before the coin was taken, but she could have gone back. Was she desperate enough to take the Copper Mill coin? Or was her mother? Was Gertie avoiding talking to Kate to protect herself or her daughter? And if Gertie wasn't guilty, she must be exhausted, cleaning every day and supporting her daughter and grandson at home. Kate began to feel sorry for Gertie Crowe.

TOM'S VAN WAS PARKED in front of the shanty where he and Sheena lived. Paul stood at the front door knocking. He could hear the sounds of artillery and fighter planes, of battle going on inside the house. He knocked louder. The noise inside stopped. Tom came to the door. He had a soda can in one hand.

"Hey, Preach, how're you doing? Come on in." Tom gave him a half smile and stood back to let Paul in.

An electric space heater sat in the corner, blowing out heat that barely made a dent in the frigid room. Tom didn't seem to notice.

"I'm doing fine, Tom, but I was concerned about you. Kate said you left rather suddenly today. Are you all right?"

"Yeah, I'm fine. I had to go to Pine Ridge. Come see what I got. The new Xbox came out today. I was afraid I wouldn't get one. These things sell out so fast, I had to get up there." He grinned and turned to let Paul see his new toy.

"It's way better than the last one I had before we moved. I got the newest war game too. You want to play?" He held out the game's controller, then took a swig of soda.

"No, thanks. You know, I'd really like to get my workbench finished. When can you come work on it?"

"I'll be there tomorrow. Shouldn't take that long."

"What time? I'll be there to help you."

"I dunno. Ten thirty or eleven, I guess."

"Kate is taking Sheena to Pine Ridge tomorrow morning. Why don't you bring her over to the house about nine? They can go, and you and I can work on the garage."

"Nine? That's too early. Make it ten."

Paul studied the young man for a moment, unsure how to respond. Tom kept glancing at his Xbox. Paul didn't know much about video games, but he knew the game system wasn't cheap.

"Try to come earlier. And bring along that list you're putting together of your experience and qualifications so we can work on your résumé."

"Sure. I'll do that." Tom took another swig of his soda.

"All right. I'll see you first thing tomorrow." There wasn't anything more he could say.

Paul could hear the artillery fire as he walked back to his car. He sat behind the wheel wondering what he could have said or done to make a difference.

"I need your help with this, Lord. I thought this was a lesson in patience for me, but it goes beyond that. My patience isn't going to help Tom take responsibility for himself and his family and get a job. Show me how I can make a difference in Tom's life. Help me to see him from your perspective, through your eyes. Amen."

Paul's discouragement lifted with his prayer. He drove home with a sense of anticipation. He didn't know how the Lord was going to work this out, but he knew God had brought this young couple into their lives for a reason. He just prayed that he and Kate would be sensitive to the Lord's leading.

Chapter Eighteen

After Paul's description of his encounter with Tom, Kate was surprised when the van pulled up at nine o'clock on the dot Tuesday morning. Paul was in his study working on his sermon notes. Kate was dressed and ready for her outing with Sheena.

"Good morning," she said, smiling as she opened the door. "Hang up your coats and come on in. I'll get Paul." She left them in the entry and went into Paul's study.

"You'll never guess who's here," she said in a hushed voice.

He looked up from his work. He couldn't see the front door from his desk. "Who?" When she grinned, he looked surprised. "Tom?"

She nodded. "Whatever you said last night must have made an impression."

"I didn't say anything." Paul marked his place and closed his Bible and notebook, then stood. "Thank you, Lord," he whispered just loud enough for Kate to hear before he went to the living room.

"Phew, I hate that smell," Sheena said, scrunching her nose as she and Kate walked along the Pine Ridge Hospital corridor. "It's so—I don't know—antiseptic."

Kate smiled. "Hospitals do have a unique scent."

They reached the maternity ward, and the antiseptic smells gave way to the pleasant scents of baby powder and baby lotion. The sounds of infant cries could be heard. Sheena looked around with curiosity. Kate stopped and tapped on a door.

"Come in."

Kate entered the room and smiled at the girl in the bed. "Hi, Wendy. I brought a friend to meet you. This is Sheena Perry. She and her husband just moved to Copper Mill."

Wendy smiled and pushed to sit up straighter. The head of the bed was raised about halfway. Wendy was wearing a blue-patterned nightgown. Her hair was flattened in the back and stuck up.

"Hi, Sheena. I'm glad you came. I'm about to go stir-crazy in here."

Kate came around to the side of the bed. "I brought you some things to help pass the time." She opened her tote bag and took out a smaller sack. "Here are novels, a book of word puzzles, and a coloring book and crayons."

"Sweet. I love to color!"

"Me too," Sheena said. She'd come to stand beside Kate. "I have something for you too." Sheena opened her shoulder pack and took out a small bracelet of blue, purple, and orange beads. She handed it to Wendy. "It's elastic, so it'll slide over your hand."

"Oh wow. That's cool," Wendy said, her eyes lighting up.

Sheena laughed. "Thanks. I hope it'll cheer you up."

Wendy pulled the bracelet over her hand, then held it up to admire it. "Sure will." Then she scrunched her nose in a look of distaste and rubbed her hand over her hair. "Sorry I look so awful. I washed my hair in the shower, but I didn't have any way to fix it."

"I can braid it for you," Sheena said, moving forward.

"Would you? That'd be great. Thanks."

"I'll do French braids on the sides so you won't have to lay on a bump." Sheena dug around in a bedside drawer and found a brush and some hair bands and started in.

"Sheena makes beautiful jewelry like the bracelet she gave you," Kate said to Wendy. "We're going to see if some of the stores in town will take them on consignment."

"Neat. I'd love to do something like that so I could work at home after the baby's born." She patted her huge, protruding abdomen. "Hey. I've got good news!" she said, beaming. "Billy got a job."

"That's wonderful!" Kate said. "Where's he working?"

"Here. Right here at the hospital. He got tired of sitting around here, so he went out and helped the nurses fix something. He just started helping, and the hospital hired him as a maintenance man. He wears a uniform, and he comes around on his breaks to see me. He's going to get benefits and everything."

"That's a real answer to prayer," Kate said, smiling. "Paul and I have been praying for Billy and Tom—Sheena's husband —to find jobs, and also for you and the baby."

Wendy's eyes widened. "Yeah. I've been praying too. It must

be working. I called and talked to my parents. Mom's going to come early, and they didn't say anything bad about Billy."

"I'm glad. I'm sure they'll be proud of him working."

Sheena looked up at Kate at that pronouncement, but she didn't say anything. She kept weaving strands of hair into a French braid. When she finished, the braids came down to Wendy's shoulders. Sheena secured them with the bands. "There. That should hold for a week at least."

Wendy flipped up the top of the bedside tray, revealing a mirror. She peered at her reflection, turning her head from side to side, then looked up at Sheena.

"Thanks. That's a huge improvement," she said. "My face doesn't look so fat this way. Billy will sure be surprised."

Her face was pleasantly rounded. Since Kate hadn't seen Wendy before her pregnancy, she didn't know if the girl's face was normally a bit chubby. Wendy's hands looked puffy, which was probably one of the reasons they wanted her to stay on bed rest.

"I know you feel self-conscious, but you look beautiful and radiant," Kate said. "I'm sure Billy sees you that way. After all, you're about to have a miracle, and he's going to be a daddy."

Wendy grinned. "Weird, isn't it. I still can't believe it." She looked down at her tummy, then back at Kate. "Billy will be a good daddy." She giggled. "He says our kids won't get away with anything 'cause he knows every trick they'll try to pull."

Wendy looked happier and livelier by the time they left. Kate and Sheena stopped to look in at the babies in the nursery.

"They're so wrinkly and red," Sheena said. Then she

laughed. "The babies in ads are so cute and cuddly. Not at all like those babies."

Kate grinned. All they could see were little faces that screwed up and turned red when they cried. "In a few days, those babies will fill out. God makes moms and dads and grand-parents blind to the wrinkles, though. All babies are beautiful."

"Yeah." Sheena got a dreamy look on her face, which faded as she thought about it. "Tom says we can't afford a baby yet. Then he goes and . . ." She stopped and pressed her lips together. Whatever she was thinking went unspoken.

"THESE ARE ALL THE RAGE. I've sold a lot of them," Sheena told the manager of the small, trendy dress shop on the refur-bished Main Street in Pine Ridge. The beautifully restored brick buildings with wrought-iron trim, scrolled moldings, and stucco friezes gave the town the ambience of wealth and the glory days of mining. As a supply town for the copper mines in the area, Pine Ridge had prospered.

"I don't think they're exactly what my clientele want, but I could take two necklaces and earrings on consignment," the manager said.

"I hope you'll be surprised. I can leave more."

"No. I'll call you if I need more." The woman clearly doubted that would be the case.

Sheena gave her a bright smile and handed her two of each. The woman wrote up a consignment agreement, and they both signed it.

Sheena received similar responses in several stores. At noon, she and Kate stopped for lunch at a café.

After they ordered, Sheena stirred her drink with a straw and stared out the window. She sighed. "I was hoping to get more orders. I know they'll sell if they'd give them a chance."

"Perhaps they will. They can call you for more if they run out."

"Yeah." She gave her head a toss. "It's all good," she said brightly.

A little too brightly, Kate thought. Something was bothering Sheena. More than discouragement that she hadn't placed more jewelry.

After lunch they crossed the street and went down the other side. Sheena placed several pieces in one store. The owner suggested they go to an area across town where an antique dealer had created an indoor mall with antique booths and artisan booths. Sheena put her merchandise in the car, and Kate drove to the old converted warehouse.

"This is cool," Sheena said as they entered the large old building.

Kate looked around while they searched for the owner. She saw several items that would look particularly nice in her home, but she resisted. She didn't need any more knickknacks.

The owner was a young woman dressed very much like Sheena, in a long, gauzy skirt and a T-shirt. She gushed over Sheena's jewelry and wanted to buy them all.

Kate wandered off, leaving the two women to discuss business while she looked through the antiques. She found a locked case with a pile of shiny old coins. Her interest piqued, she bent down and studied the collection. There were Civil War tokens and Confederate coins and lots of old copper pennies and Indian-head nickels.

The coins had been polished, which made them look attractive and expensive, although Kate doubted they were very valuable. Surely the proprietor wouldn't leave them in such a vulnerable place if they were, unless she didn't realize their value.

Kate looked for the Copper Mill coin. She spotted a couple of old silver dollars, but nothing resembling the missing copper coin. She hadn't expected to find it. After all, what good would the coin do a thief if it was tossed into a pile of junk coins?

Kate went back up front to wait for Sheena. She didn't want to hurry her, but Kate was antsy to get home and continue her search for Skip. It might take a bit of digging, but that didn't bother her. She had to find him.

"She took almost everything!" Sheena said as they returned to Kate's car. "She loves my jewelry!" Sheena twirled around in a circle.

"That's wonderful. I hope they sell really well."

"Me too," Sheena said, her eyes shining.

As they drove toward the edge of town, Sheena spotted the SuperMart.

"Can we stop there, Kate? I need to look at computers."

"All right." Kate pulled into the parking lot. "Are you thinking about buying a computer?"

"Yeah. I need one so I can sell my beads and jewelry over the Internet. I can't afford the one I really want, but I've got to start somewhere."

Kate put the car in park and turned to Sheena. "Having a computer won't necessarily help you."

Sheena turned to her, her eyes wide. "Why not? I can't sell them unless I have a Web site and access to the Internet."

"I sell my stained-glass creations on the Internet, and I don't have good access to the Internet at home. All you can get is dial-up, which is very slow, unless you spend the money to get broadband or a satellite dish. Then the monthly costs are pretty high. I go to the library and use their computers for free. I have a simple Web site. Sometimes I list things on eBay. You could do that too."

Sheena's mouth drooped. "But I *need* a computer. Tom went and bought an Xbox and used *my* credit card. Now it's almost maxed out. If I don't get this now, he'll buy something else, and I won't have enough credit." She sighed as if defeated.

"Sheena, I'll be happy to help you get started selling on the Internet through the library."

Sheena's shoulders sagged. She looked ready to cry. "I guess you're right," she said. "I guess I don't need to stop here."

Kate reached over and patted Sheena's hand, then she put the car in gear and drove out of the parking lot, silently praying as she turned onto the road to Copper Mill. *Lord, please help this young couple. They need your wisdom and guidance and hope.*

TOM TIGHTENED THE LAST SCREW attaching the workbench to the garage's back wall. He stood, set down his portable drill, took hold of the bench leg and wiggled it. The worktable didn't budge. Tom grinned and stood back.

"Give it a try," he said.

Paul tried to rock it, but it stood firm. "Very nice," he said, beaming at the work they'd accomplished. "All we have left is the toolholder and upper shelves, and I'll be in business," he said, rubbing his hands together.

They were admiring their work when the garage door clicked on and began to rise. Paul glanced at his watch. "It's three thirty already."

Tom began stashing his tools in the five-gallon bucket he carried with him. "Time to get going," he said. He grinned at Paul. "I got a war to win," he said with a chuckle.

"We didn't have a chance to work on your résumé. If you want to find work and make a home here, Tom, you're going to have to set some priorities and settle down. I know the video games are fun, but playing games won't help you get established. That money could have gone toward a security deposit on a rental apartment."

"No worries. I didn't spend cash. I charged it." Tom picked up his bucket and walked out to his van as Kate's car pulled into the garage.

Paul shook his head. What could he say? "Shall we plan to finish this tomorrow?" he asked.

"Not sure. I'll let you know." He stashed his bucket, then came back to Kate's car.

"How'd you do?" he asked Sheena as she got out.

"Good," she said. "I have some left, though."

"Hand 'em over. I'll put them in the van so we can get going." Sheena gave Tom the nearly empty box.

"I thought you'd sell all of these," he said.

She gave him an exasperated look. "I'm trying my best," she said.

It wasn't difficult for Paul to interpret her unspoken rebuke. She was working hard and trying to sell her jewelry. Tom wasn't working very diligently at getting a job.

Patience, he reminded himself. *Patience*.

WEDNESDAY MORNING, Kate was at the library, armed with a list of questions and search words, when Livvy opened up.

"Morning," Livvy said, pushing the door open. "You look like you're freezing."

Kate laughed. "What gave me away? My rosy cheeks, my blue lips, or the icicles I'm exhaling?"

"How about the frost on your eyelashes?"

"You're kidding, aren't you?" Kate batted her eyes. They didn't clink or break off. She clapped her gloved hands together to warm them.

"Come in. I just started a pot of coffee. I'll give you a cup to warm up. How's the investigation going?"

"I'm hoping for a real breakthrough today. And a cup of coffee sounds wonderful."

"Since you're the only one here, and I know you're careful, you can take it upstairs with you."

"Bless you," Kate said, smiling as she followed her friend to the employees' break room.

Kate knew the library frowned on eating and drinking in the public areas, so Livvy's offer was especially nice. She took the cup upstairs and went to the last computer so she'd be out of the way when other patrons arrived.

Kate started at the top of her list, running a search for Griff Henley. Pages and pages of references popped onto the screen. *Dr. Griffith A. Henley, professor emeritus*. The man had articles in several prestigious academic publications. According to the titles, his topics covered the history of natural-resource development, specifically mining, mostly in the South in the nineteenth century. Impressive, but that didn't make him immune to temptation. No wonder he was interested in Joshua Parsons' stories about local mining.

She found a link to G. A. Henley's personal Web site. It identified him as a professor of history at Wesleyan University. It had to be Joshua Parsons' niece's husband.

Kate followed a link to Henley's private collection. Several pages showed old books, mining memorabilia, black-and-white and sepia-toned photographs of mines and miners, and pictures of buttons and tokens, assay reports, and mine claims. She looked for the coin but didn't see it pictured. If Griff had taken it, he hadn't posted it on his Web site.

Kate followed another link to Henley's Web log. Excited, she read a post dated Friday of the previous week. He described a trip he'd taken tracing the Old Copper Road along the Ocoee River. He included several photographs of his tour. One picture showed the group, including Griff and Eloise Henley, in front of a sign to the Old Copper Road. There was snow on the ground, obliterating the trail. It was definitely the group from the Hamilton Springs Hotel.

Going back through several blog entries, Kate found mention of the Old Copper commemorative coin. The entry was dated the previous Tuesday, five days after she'd discovered the coin was missing. She paused to read the blog. It showed a hazy picture of Copper Mill's coin taken through the display-case glass and describing the mining celebration when the coin was unveiled. The account read like the old newspaper article in the display case. *Nothing incriminating here, but why no mention that the coin's missing?* Kate wondered.

The photograph was taken before the coin disappeared.

Surely Griff knows that the coin was stolen. Or doesn't he consider that important enough news to include in his blog?

Kate clicked on the comments to the blog. Digger Dan wrote that his uncle worked in the Burra Burra Mine and described visiting there and collecting garnets as a child. Another post decried the environmental damage to the landscape around copper mines. A third post wanted to know more about the coin and its value.

Kate perked up. The question came from "Anonymous." Griff's response was interesting. One word. *Priceless.*

Who is Anonymous? Evelyn or Georgia Cline perhaps? Or could it be Gertie or Prissy?

Kate decided to post her own comment and see if it raised a response.

I would love to purchase a medallion like the one pictured for my collection of exonumia. Do you know how many were minted and if there are any available?

Kate signed it "Interested Party." And she *was* interested. She didn't personally collect coins, but Paul had his father's coin collection somewhere still packed away. Kate remembered seeing it in San Antonio before they moved to Tennessee. She didn't know where it was at the moment, but it was in a box somewhere at their house. Besides, what if someone responded to her query, trying to sell the coin—the stolen one. And how would they know? Unless it was one of her suspects.

Kate noted the Web URL for Griff's blog, then went on to another search. She typed in "classic car restorers, Florida."

A mishmash of links came up, including many sites selling classic cars. She tried to narrow the search to classic trucks in Florida, hoping to eliminate some of the listings. Sites came up linking to sales, parts, shows, collections, models, books, and manuals.

She scrolled through several pages, finally linking to a classified listing of restoration businesses. Kate had to decide whether to search for engine repairs, interior restoration, or bodywork. She guessed that Skip's chief concern would be bodywork, since he could clean out the inside, and he'd been working on the engine with Jim Hepburn.

She followed several links to *Body Shops in Northern Florida* and wrote down the phone numbers and Web site addresses in case she needed to look them up again.

Shutting down the computer, Kate walked out of the library and headed to the Mercantile. Her mother had always said you could catch more flies with honey than with vinegar. Kate believed it, and she had some catching to do.

Chapter Nineteen

Kate considered deep-frying the chicken Southern-style but decided to cook her oven-fried version instead. It was healthier, and she wouldn't have to stand over the stove while it cooked.

She put potatoes on to boil, then made two piecrusts. She couldn't make a pie to give away without making one for Paul.

While the pecan pies baked, Kate sat at the counter with her notebook and started making phone calls to Florida auto body shops.

The first call received a curt reply. The man wasn't working on any pickup trucks and hadn't talked to anyone from Tennessee. Kate thanked him, hung up, and crossed him off her list.

Most of her calls received polite but negative answers. She got additional leads, however, so her search wasn't completely fruitless.

The potatoes started to boil over. Kate turned them to low and made another call. A jovial man with a Texas accent answered. When he heard her accent, he wanted to chat with a fellow Texan. He'd retired to Florida and did bodywork as a hobby out of his converted garage.

Kate learned that Skip's truck wasn't likely worth much. She discovered some years were more valuable than others. She didn't find Skip, but she gained a whole list of retirees who were restoring their own classics and taking on occasional jobs to fund their restorations.

Kate set the list aside while she fixed the chicken. While it baked, she made coleslaw. It was three o'clock by the time Kate packed the meal in a basket, still hot and ready for delivery.

GERTIE'S DOUBLEWIDE MOBILE HOME sat back off of Barnhill Street, about a mile out of town. There weren't any other houses around. She turned into the dirt driveway at the mailbox marked Crowe and drove back to a copse of trees. A pergola covered with wisteria vines provided a shaded porch on the front of the trailer. Two flowerpots with the dry skeletons of geraniums sat on either side of the door.

Kate didn't see a car, but she heard the sounds of cartoons coming from inside. She set her basket down and knocked on the door.

Prissy opened the door. "Yes?" she said.

The cartoon sounds got louder.

"Hi. I'm Kate Hanlon. Arlene introduced us at the post office. Is your mother at home?"

"Oh yeah. I remember. She's working in Pine Ridge."

"Oh. I heard that she didn't come to work at Town Hall yesterday, so I was concerned that she might not be feeling well. I brought you some dinner." Kate lifted the basket. "It's chicken and all the trimmings, and a pecan pie for dessert."

She passed the basket to Prissy, who looked stunned. Kate gave her a sweet smile. "Would you tell your mother I came by? I left my name and phone number in the basket. I'd like to talk to her."

"Ah, sure. Th-thanks, um, Kate."

KATE SPENT A GOOD PART of Thursday trying to track Skip down. By midafternoon, she'd talked to just about every body shop and mechanic in the northern half of Florida and left messages at others. No one had called her back.

One call left to make, then she'd have to tackle the southern half. A lady answered. Her husband had recently passed away. She gave Kate the number of a retired navy chief who operated a small shop outside Pensacola and worked on vehicles for navy personnel. Kate doubted the referral would help, but she couldn't reject even the tiniest possibility. She called.

"This is Sandy. Can't come to the phone right now. Leave me a message." The voice was gravelly but pleasant.

With a sigh, Kate waited for the beep. "This is Kate Hanlon from Copper Mill, Tennessee. I'm looking for Skip Spencer. He might be getting work done on his 1969 blue Ford F-100 Ranger pickup. If his truck is in your shop, please have him call Sheriff Roberts or me." Kate repeated her phone number and the sheriff's office number twice.

Certain the message was a waste of time, Kate headed to the library for a more extensive list. This time she would include mechanics, but she had no guarantee that Skip had taken his truck to anyone. It was a hunch. A proverbial shot in the dark.

AT THE LIBRARY, Kate printed out a list of auto body shops and mechanics in southern Florida, although she doubted Skip would have gone that far away to have his truck restored. She wished Jayme Johnson had told her where she lived. Was she protecting herself or Skip?

Kate found nearly two hundred Jayme Johnsons online. Four were in Florida. She would have to subscribe to a service to get the phone numbers, and Kate didn't feel quite right about breaching someone's privacy that way, even though the numbers were available. She'd given the information to the sheriff so he could pursue it if he wished. Kate decided to keep that option as a last resort.

Next, Kate went to Griff Henley's blog to see if her questions about the commemorative coin had elicited a response, and she wasn't disappointed. A response from Anonymous indicated an interest in buying or bidding on a coin that commemorated the Copper Road, if any were available. So someone else wanted it. But that someone was a buyer, not the thief.

The blog for the day reported the theft of the Copper Mill commemorative coin and the tragedy of pilfered antiquities. Griff gave examples of ancient civilizations whose graves and town sites had been looted by private collectors and people out for a quick buck. Something as insignificant as a penny coin could date a discovery. Removing it might eradicate that knowledge.

Griff stated firmly that he had no knowledge of who owned any of the limited edition coins, and his only interest would be in restoring it to the town as part of its heritage. He wrote that if anyone knew where the stolen coin might be, they should call the Harrington County Sheriff. Kate wanted to applaud his sentiments. Although his post wasn't proof positive of his innocence, she considered it unlikely he'd been involved. But that didn't rule out the others in his group.

FRIDAY MORNING, Kate woke refreshed and eager to begin the day. A new layer of snow covered the lawn and flocked the trees. Kate loved it. She started the coffee, then laid a fire in the fireplace before settling into her favorite chair with her coffee and her Bible.

A verse from some recent reading or sermon was on the edge of her mind, just out of reach. Something about time. Something about God's timing. Something about overcoming trials or an enemy. She looked in the Psalms but couldn't find the passage, so she started to pray. Giving her burden to the Lord, Kate prayed again that she would learn who had stolen the coin and prove Skip's innocence.

She was just finishing and closed her Bible when Paul came out to the living room with a cup of coffee and his Bible and sat across from her. He leaned forward, his Bible in his lap. He had a look of excitement that was at odds with his sleep-ruffled hair.

"I have to read this to you," he said, opening his Bible and flipping through the pages. "I started studying last week for the sermon series I want to do, and something you said about us suddenly being the wiser, older mentors struck a chord with me. I didn't know what I was supposed to see, but I knew God was leading me somewhere. Then I forgot about it as we got involved in Tom and Sheena's lives. I just found it. Here it is:

I will stand at my watch and station myself on the ramparts; I will look to see what he will say to me, and what answer I am to give to this complaint.

Then the Lord replied: "Write down the revelation and make it plain on tablets so that a herald may run with it. For the revelation awaits an appointed time; it speaks of the end and will not prove false. Though it linger, wait for it; it will certainly come and will not delay."

The words struck Kate as if God had sent them just for her. "That last part, that's what I was looking for. Where is that?"

"Habakkuk 2:1–3," Paul said. "I kept thinking the Lord was trying to teach me patience. I've certainly had to exercise it with Tom. But the Lord was telling me to stand my watch and wait to hear what answer he wants to share with Tom."

"I was thinking about that yesterday," Kate said. "I've called just about every auto body shop in Florida without success. I've been trying so hard to find Skip, I forgot to wait and see what God's going to do."

"He's never late."

"He's never late. I'll try to remember that," Kate said, willing herself to repeat it and believe it.

THOSE WORDS REPLAYED over and over in Kate's mind after Paul left for the church later that morning. Tom didn't show up to work in the garage again. They hadn't seen or heard from him since he and Sheena left Tuesday afternoon, but Kate didn't fret about it. She and Paul had prayed, turning Skip and Tom and Sheena over to the Lord to await his timing.

Kate knew that God was talking to Habakkuk in the passage Paul read, not to Kate Hanlon, but the timeless message was for her. The prophet had talked to God, trying to understand God's plan. He determined to stand watch and wait on the Lord, and he got his answer. God told him to write it all down, then wait for the right time to reveal it.

She sat at the kitchen table with her notepad and wrote down every detail that she'd learned about Skip, the coin, and everyone who might have a motive to take it. She'd concluded that Evelyn and Georgia Cline, Gertie Crowe, and perhaps her daughter Prissy had reason to want the coin. She added Griff Henley as a person of interest, but she doubted his involvement after following his blog comments. Tom and Sheena had also viewed the coin and been told of its importance and value.

Even with a list of alternate suspects, the circumstantial evidence against Skip still looked convicting. Kate hated to admit that a few doubts had crept into her mind. At the very least, Skip had a lot of explaining to do.

Unhappy with her thoughts, Kate set the notepad aside and left the puzzle in God's hands. Perhaps working on Valentine cards would free her thoughts. Sometimes solutions occurred when she turned to another task.

She'd barely sat down at the kitchen table when the doorbell rang. Setting the cards aside, she went to the door. Sheena stood there looking miserable, her eyes red rimmed.

"Come in. What's wrong?"

"Ooh, Kate." Sheena burst into tears and threw her arms around Kate's neck, sobbing against her shoulder.

Kate patted the young woman's shoulders and smoothed her hair like she would a little child's.

She took Sheena's hands, pulling her toward the kitchen. "Come on. Come sit down and tell me what's wrong."

She guided Sheena to the table and handed her a box of tissues. Then she sat across from her and waited.

"I'm so-o-rry," Sheena wailed.

She sniffled and blew her nose. Her breathing came out in little hiccups. Finally she calmed down and her breathing slowed, but the anguish in her eyes broke Kate's heart. She couldn't imagine the tragedy Sheena was facing to cause such grief. She reached out and took hold of Sheena's hands. Sheena sniffed and tried to smile. Fresh tears spilled over.

"We . . . we had a fight," she managed to say. She pursed her lips together. Her chin quivered. Her hands trembled.

Kate patted her hands. "I'm sorry," she said. "Take a deep breath while I get you a cup of tea. Then we can talk." Kate smiled kindly.

Sheena nodded and wiped her eyes with a tissue.

Kate handed Sheena a damp dishcloth. The young woman held it over her swollen eyes. Her crying subsided, and she calmed down while Kate made two cups of tea. Kate set one cup in front of Sheena, then sat down facing her and waited.

"Thank you." Sheena gave Kate a small smile. "I had to talk to someone."

Kate nodded and sipped her tea.

Sheena took a sip, then set the cup down and stared into it as she cradled it between her hands. "We argued over money and work. I told him he shouldn't have bought an

Xbox when he couldn't pay for it, and he should be looking for a job instead of playing stupid games. He called me a nag and said I don't understand that he needs to get his mind off his troubles. Well, they're my troubles too. I told him I need a computer to help make money, and he said nobody would buy my stuff." Fresh tears sprang to her eyes. She dabbed at them.

"That hurt." Sheena shook her head, sending her hair flying back and forth. "It got worse from there. We were yelling at each other, and he told me to leave him alone, so I did."

She looked up, beseeching Kate to understand and sympathize with her. "I didn't know where else to go."

"You're welcome here anytime. Relationships are hard sometimes. At one time or another, we all make unwise choices and say things we don't mean."

"Yeah, well, I meant it. He isn't even trying to get a job. Not very hard anyways. That's what makes me so mad. He's a good carpenter. He knows I want a house and kids. I can't make enough to save up a deposit and two months' rent, though. Especially when he goes and uses the credit card."

"You're both angry. That will pass, but the hurt won't go away unless you forgive each other and work together to solve your problems."

"Forgive each other? I didn't do anything wrong."

"I know it doesn't seem that way, but arguments are usually two-sided."

Sheena shook her head.

Kate thought a moment before she said anything more. She didn't want to push too hard. "I remember when Paul and I were first married. He didn't make much money as an assistant pastor. Our church was small. But I was working and I'd been used to spending my own money to buy whatever I wanted. I saw a beautiful dress in Talbots, so I bought it." Kate chuckled. "I think it cost me a whole week's wages. And I didn't consult with Paul. Never even occurred to me to ask him about it first."

"But it was just a dress," Sheena said, giving Kate a perplexed look.

"True. But I didn't need it. I just wanted it. I wore it to church. Paul never said a word, but I overheard two of the older ladies criticize me to him for wasting our money on frivolous things. I was shocked. Then he stood up for me, gently suggesting they shouldn't judge me. At first I was indignant, but then I realized I never considered that we were a team and it was our money, not mine or his."

"Yeah. Tom doesn't think about that either," Sheena said.

Kate didn't remind Sheena that she'd claimed what she earned as her money when she wanted to buy a computer. "Paul and I started praying together for our marriage and for our lives to reflect God's love. I was amazed how that made a difference. We became a team working toward our goals. Maybe you and Tom could sit down together and talk about your finances."

"I know we need to do that, but I'm afraid we'll end up arguing again."

Kate thought that was likely unless they could face their struggles together instead of competing with each other. "Have you ever prayed for Tom?" she asked.

Sheena looked panicked at the suggestion. "Me pray? I don't . . ." She shifted in her chair. "I'm not good at praying. Do you think God really listens?"

"Absolutely. I know he does. He answers too. Not always the way we want, but the way that is best."

"I never thought about that, but I could try," she said hesitantly.

"I think God would be pleased to hear from you. Sheena, does Tom know you're here?"

"No. I grabbed the keys and left."

"Why don't you call him and let him know where you are so he won't worry. Then if you'd like, you can help me make apricot-nut bread for the Faith Freezer Program. Would you like to help?"

"Sure. What's the Faith Freezer Program?"

Kate explained the meals program, then left Sheena to call Tom. She carried their empty teacups to the sink, silently praying that Tom's temper had cooled, and he'd want to reconcile with his unhappy wife. She went out to the garage, giving Sheena privacy on the phone.

When Kate came back in, Sheena was still on the telephone. She didn't hear yelling, so that was good. She sorted through some old newspapers. There were a couple of articles she wanted to read later, so she set them next to the couch. Sheena came into the living room.

"He said he's sorry. I'm going back home now. Thanks for the help."

KATE SENT SHEENA HOME with a loaf of banana bread from her freezer to put Tom in a good mood and ease their reunion. She was writing a note in a Valentine card when her cell phone rang. She picked it up and looked at it. She recognized the Florida prefix.

"Hello, this is Kate Hanlon," she answered.

"Missus Hanlon, it's Skip Spencer."

Relief flooded through her at the sound of his deep voice.

"I got a message to call you or the sheriff. Is something wrong with my mom?" he asked.

"Other than that she's worried about you? No, she's fine. You haven't called the sheriff then?"

"Not yet. I thought I'd call you first. I imagine he's ticked at me for leaving work."

"Ticked doesn't cover it, Skip. Where are you? Are you okay?"

"I'm fine. My cell phone died the first day, and I forgot my charger, so I haven't been able to call anyone. Then I got busy. I forgot my mom would be worried."

Kate remembered seeing the charger at his apartment. No wonder he hadn't returned any of her calls.

"I'll call her," he said. "I can't make it home until Monday."

"Skip, you need to get home sooner." She took a deep breath. "The day you disappeared, Copper Mill's prized commemorative coin from the display case at Town Hall also disappeared."

"Yikes. Have they caught the thief?"

"I'm afraid not. Skip, the investigation points to you. The sheriff has a warrant out for your arrest. You—"

"H-h-he what?" Skip's voice rose almost an octave.

"You need to call him and get home immediately."

Kate heard a heavy sigh, then silence.

"I didn't take the coin."

"I believe you, Skip. I've been trying to prove that."

"I-if you can't prove it, I'm in r-real trouble, aren't I?"

"All the evidence is circumstantial. There's no proof that you did take it, Skip."

"What can I do to prove I had nothing to do with it?"

"Call the sheriff and get here as soon as you can. Do you have a phone number where we can reach you?"

"You can leave messages at the auto shop like you did." He repeated the number.

"I'll have to tell the sheriff I talked to you, Skip. You'd better call him now so he hears it from you first."

"All right. Th-thanks, Missus Hanlon . . . for everything." The line went dead.

Chapter Twenty

K ate baked four loaves of bread for Faith Freezer, and then packed up a box of stained-glass candleholders and garden stakes to deliver to Smith Street Gifts. After she dropped them off, she drove by Town Hall. The sheriff's SUV was parked in front of the building. As Kate entered Town Hall, she heard Sheriff Roberts' voice coming from the open door of the deputy's office. She went straight to the office. The sheriff's back was to the door.

"Good afternoon, Sheriff. Deputy Martin. Have you heard from Skip?"

The men turned their heads toward her.

"No. Have you?" the sheriff asked.

"Yes. I thought he would have called you by now."

The sheriff whipped around to face Kate. "Where is he?"

"In Florida. I tracked body shops in Florida. One of them has his truck. I left a message and Skip just called me. I told him to contact you and to get home immediately. He had no idea the coin was stolen. I told him to hurry back. He said he can't get here until Monday."

"Monday? Where in Florida? Perhaps I should go down there to apprehend him myself."

"That's up to you, but I think he'll come home. He's concerned about his mother..." Kate's voice trailed off as the telephone rang.

The deputy picked it up. He answered, then held out the phone to the sheriff.

The sheriff gave Kate a look that told her to stay put, then he answered the phone.

"Sheriff Roberts here." He listened for a few moments. "Spencer, you get your..." He glanced at Kate. "Give Deputy Martin your contact information, then get back to Copper Mill ASAP, or I'll come down and get you."

The sheriff handed the phone to Hugh. The deputy sat down at the desk and started writing down the information from Skip.

The sheriff turned back to Kate. "He said he tried calling me earlier. I didn't get the message. Thanks, Kate. I'll give him until Monday evening to show up. If he doesn't, I'll have him picked up."

Kate frowned. "I don't have proof of his innocence yet. Hopefully he can clear that up. I found a blog on the Internet that might be of interest." She told the sheriff about Griff Henley and the anonymous post on his blog.

"All that tells me is that the coin is valuable enough that others want it too. If Anonymous stole the coin, he wouldn't be looking for it on the Internet."

"He or she," Kate corrected. "A thief might be looking to see who's interested in buying such a coin. I'll keep following the thread."

Before she left the building, Kate looked for the cleaning lady but didn't find her. The floor had the shine of a recent cleaning, though, so Gertie was still on the job. Kate hadn't really expected to hear from the elusive woman, but she'd hoped to get past Gertie's defenses. She wondered if Gertie and Prissy had enjoyed the pie and the chicken dinner.

LATE SATURDAY MORNING, Paul held the top board in place on the back of the shelving unit while Tom used his electric drill to screw it in place, first one side, then the other. The two men were putting the finishing touches on Paul's workbench. Even though Tom had been unreliable in terms of scheduling, the young man was undeniably talented.

Tom picked up a second board and held it to the bottom of the shelving unit. Paul leaned down and held the board securely while Tom drilled the screws in place, then he straightened up to trade places.

"So how goes the job search?" Paul asked as he moved to the other end.

Tom raised the drill and looked at him. "Didn't have time to look this week."

"That's a shame. I talked to Doug Campbell for you, by the way. He was awarded a contract to put up a strip mall outside Pine Ridge. He's going to need reliable men."

Tom lowered the drill and set the screw into the wood. He immediately moved on to the next screw. Then he stood. "Gotta get this job finished first."

Paul felt like he might as well be hammering his head against the wall. It would accomplish about as much as trying to talk to Tom.

Lord, help me out here. What can I say? How can I help Tom if he doesn't want to help himself?

Tom straddled the shelving unit, fingering the drill trigger, whirling it on, then off, then on as he contemplated the floor. Finally he stopped and looked at Paul. "I suppose I could help him out for a while, until I get on my feet, but I plan to be bidding against him, not working for him."

"That's a good dream, Tom. But dreams are just vapors in the air if you don't put substance behind them. What are you willing to do to make your dream a reality?"

Tom stared at him with a blank expression.

He doesn't get it, Paul thought.

Tom picked up a piece of fiberboard and laid it against the back of the shelf. "You want to hold this while I screw it in place?"

"Sure." Paul leaned over and held the board in place.

Tom went around putting screws in along the edge. At the second to last screw, the drill went dead. It wouldn't start.

Tom let slip an unintelligible sound of disgust. He set the drill down hard.

"That's just great," he said, planting his hands on his hips.

Paul almost smiled, but he refrained. "Hold on."

A regular screwdriver would do the trick, but Tom needed an object lesson, and Paul wasn't about to pass up an opportunity. He went over to the side of the garage where his truck had been parked and shuffled through a stack of boxes. He found one marked Dad's Tools that he hadn't opened yet. He carried it over to the new workbench and set it down, then opened it.

Paul began taking out the contents of the box, looking for

a specific tool. He took out a small, ornately carved wooden box. He recognized the box. He'd wondered which box he'd packed it in. He set it on the counter to deal with later. The tool he wanted was underneath.

"Here's what we need," he said. "An old-fashioned Yankee-ratchet screwdriver." He pulled out a long wood-handled screwdriver.

"I know this isn't the latest in technology, but it's reliable. Unlike battery-powered tools, this little tool doesn't need electricity. It just needs manpower. Watch this." He set the tip on the screw head and pushed down on the knob. The tip twisted. In seconds, the screw was firmly embedded.

"Cool. Let me try it." Tom picked up the old tool and quickly finished the job.

"We're like that portable drill, Tom. We get plugged into the wrong power source, or we don't bother to plug in or show up, and we just sputter and run out of juice. Proverbs 28:19–20 says, 'He who works his land will have abundant food, but the one who chases fantasies will have his fill of poverty. A faithful man will be richly blessed, but one eager to get rich will not go unpunished.'"

Tom listened politely. He nodded his head. "Yeah. So I need to get rid of my rechargeable tools and get manual ones. Is that it?"

Is he dense or just purposely ignoring the point? Paul shook his head. He put the screwdriver away, then reached for the carved wooden box, but he didn't quite get a firm grip on it. The box teetered on the edge of the countertop and fell, cracking the top and falling open, spilling its contents all over the floor.

He dropped down to his knees to pick up dozens of old coins from his father's coin collection. There were Indian-head nickels and copper pennies and old dimes and quarters and a few Liberty silver dollars. If Paul remembered correctly, there were several coins that were very old and perhaps valuable.

Tom dropped down to help him.

"Man, these are old," he said, holding one up, then turning it over. "Must be a fortune here."

"They belonged to my father," Paul said. "That's their value."

Tom gave him an incredulous look. Evidently he had no idea what sentimental value meant. They gathered them all, then Paul carried the box inside to go through later. The coins didn't belong in a box of tools.

He set the coin box on the table by the couch, next to magazines and a box of craft items that Kate had left on the table. So much for trying to impart some wisdom. With a sigh, Paul returned to the garage. Tom had moved the box of tools and was sweeping up the bits of wood shavings they'd created.

KATE WAS IRONING in the bedroom and hated to stop for lunch, but there were two hungry guys in the garage. She turned off the iron and went to the kitchen, where she threw together a quick soup from leftover chicken, rice, vegetables, and some diced andouille sausage in chicken broth. She grilled cheese-and-tomato sandwiches and called the men to eat.

After lunch, the men went to the garage. Kate put away the lunch fixings, then returned to the bedroom to finish the ironing.

She was carrying a stack of Valentine cards from her studio

to the kitchen when she heard a car pull into the driveway. She set the cards down on a table in the living room and opened the door just as the doorbell rang.

"Dolores. Trixie. Come in." Kate took their coats and hung them on the coat tree. They removed their shoes and left them with their handbags by the door. Dolores looked gaunt and pale, with dark circles under her eyes. Trixie looked tired.

Hammering sounds came from the garage. Kate led the ladies to the kitchen table. "I just made coffee. Have a seat, and I'll bring you a cup."

She carried a tray of goodies, cream and sugar, and cups of coffee to the table. Trixie helped herself to a cookie. Dolores accepted the coffee and slowly stirred cream into it but declined the food.

Dolores took the seat with her back to the living room, as if to hide her troubles from the world, and Trixie sat on the other side. Kate sat at the end of the table. "How are you doing?" she asked Dolores.

Dolores kept stirring her coffee, but her chin began to tremble. Kate waited, praying for the right words to comfort Skip's mother.

Finally, Dolores looked up. "Not very well. I'm sorry to bother you. I'm sure you're busy."

Kate gave her a gentle smile meant to encourage and reassure. "It's all right. I told you to come any time. I meant it. Did Skip call you?"

"Yes. He said you got ahold of him and told him what happened. He's coming home." She gave Kate a pinched smile. "Thank you for finding him. I'm relieved that he's all right, but the sheriff will arrest him as soon as he gets here," she said.

Kate nodded. Trixie sipped her coffee and took a praline. She acted distracted, as if she had other things on her mind.

"I'm glad Skip called him right away. I had no choice but to tell the sheriff that I found him," Kate said. "I hope Skip can prove his innocence."

"That's just it. He can't." Dolores dabbed at the moisture in her eyes. "I keep imagining him in handcuffs. He's so proud of his uniform and all his police gear, and now the sheriff is going to . . ." Dolores broke into sobs. "He's going to put my son in that horrible jail. I can't stand it."

Kate went to her and held her while she cried. She glanced over at Trixie, who looked very uncomfortable.

"I tried to tell her it would be all right. They can't prove anything," Trixie said in hushed tones, "but it doesn't do any good." She got up from the table. "I'm going to take my coffee into the living room so you two can spend some time talking alone."

Kate gave Trixie a little nod of approval, thinking that was very sweet and sensitive of her.

"Take your time. I'll be fine," Trixie mouthed. She took another cookie and went into the living room.

Kate saw her looking around. The room was cluttered, but it couldn't be helped. Trixie would find some magazines.

Kate pulled a chair around next to Dolores and gave her full attention to the grieving mother. "I've got several possible leads. Enough to discount the circumstantial evidence at least," Kate said.

Dolores sniffed. Her sobs subsided. She looked up at Kate with red-rimmed eyes. "What if . . . ?" She left the question unfinished.

Kate knew what she was thinking. She'd wondered herself. "Do you believe my son is innocent?" Dolores finally asked.

Did she? How could she answer honestly? "From what I know of Skip, I believe he is honest. I can't imagine him breaking the law."

Dolores' chin firmed. "Thank you, Kate. It means a lot that you believe in him. I do too, but the sheriff seems so sure, I wondered if I'm being blind because Skip's my son. The sheriff's always been fair and given Skip the benefit of the doubt when he's made mistakes before, but he told me there isn't any other explanation this time."

Kate hated to distress Dolores further by asking questions, but she saw no alternative. "Sometimes, under dire circumstances, people make bad choices and go against their character. Do you know of anything that may have been troubling Skip? Did he owe money or invest in anything?"

"No. Except . . . he was saving to fix that . . . that junker of a truck. He wouldn't steal to do that. He had almost enough money in the bank. I told him he shouldn't waste it on that rattletrap. He should buy a decent car."

Kate heard the garage door to the house open and close. Then she heard Trixie talking to someone in the living room. Paul or Tom, she assumed. With her back to the living room, she ignored the voices to concentrate on Dolores.

A knock sounded at the front door. She started to get up, but Trixie answered it. Whoever it was went away, and it got quiet again. No telling what Trixie said to the person, but she'd worry about that later.

"I just can't imagine," Dolores continued. "He's never done anything like this before."

"I'm sure he has a good reason. He had something important on his mind when I talked to him that morning." Kate heard a door open and close again. It got quiet.

"I've discovered several people who had access and possible motives for taking the coin," Kate said. "I don't know if I can prove one of them took it, but at the least, it could keep the case from going to court."

Dolores shook her head sadly. "That might keep him out of jail, but people will still wonder if he did it, and no one will want to hire him again. I'm praying for a miracle so Skip will be cleared completely."

"So am I, Dolores. And I'll do everything I can to help. I promise."

Dolores wiped at tears on her cheeks. She took a tissue from Kate and blew her nose. "Thank you, Kate, for all you've done and all you're trying to do. I'd better go now and let you get back to your day."

"Would you like me to pray with you before you go?" Kate offered.

"Yes please."

They bowed their heads, and Kate prayed for the miracle to clear Skip of all charges and for his safe return. When they finished, Dolores stood. Kate walked with her to the living room.

Trixie was leaning back on the couch, her eyes closed, softly snoring. She must have instantly fallen asleep after getting the door.

"Poor thing. She's just tuckered out," Dolores said. "She came to visit me for a vacation and got dumped right in the middle of my problems. She'll be so happy to get home."

"When does she head back?"

"Tuesday. She got a note from her son that the house will be ready. He had to go somewhere on business, but he said he'll be back in a few days. She's so excited, she already packed. I think she'd leave today, but he told her the cleaning crew won't get in there until Tuesday morning, so it'll be ready by the time she gets there."

"How is she traveling?"

"She's taking a bus. That's how she got here." Dolores went over to her friend and nudged her gently.

Trixie jerked awake. "What? What?" She sat up and looked around. "I must have fallen asleep. You have a very comfortable couch, Kate." She stood and smoothed her clothes. "Is it time to go?"

Kate walked them to the door. They gathered their belongings, Dolores hugged Kate, then they left. Kate was pleased that the worry lines on Dolores' face had smoothed, as if her burden had been lifted a little bit.

Chapter Twenty-One

No sooner did Dolores and Trixie leave than Livvy pulled up. Kate stood on the front stoop while her friend got out of her SUV and came to the door. She was carrying a pot with a bunch of little green spikes and purple buds.

"For you," she said, carrying it inside. "Grape hyacinths to prove spring will be here soon. Where shall I put them?"

"Livvy, that's just gorgeous," Kate drawled.

"Bless your heart, Kate, you look beat. I saw Dolores and Trixie leaving. You do take on the burdens of the world, don't you, girl?"

"Not any more than you or any other caring person would. And you're enough to cheer anyone. Come have coffee."

"I'd love to, but I can't stay long. Besides, I suspect your day's been interrupted enough. I hear the hammering in the garage. Is Paul finally getting his workbench finished?"

"Yes. Tom came over this morning."

"You probably have a headache by now."

"Not anymore. You just cured it." Kate poured two cups of coffee and offered Livvy a praline.

"Yum!" She took a piece and bit off a tiny bite, then followed it with a sip of coffee. "I just died and went to heaven."

"Let's sit in here. The living room's a mess."

"Phooey. Nobody pays any attention. Certainly not me."

Tom came in to get a drink of water. Kate got up and gave him a glass. She offered coffee, but he turned her down. He accepted a praline, then took his glass out to the garage.

"Anything new on Skip?" Livvy asked, switching gears.

Kate nodded. "Yes. I found him. He'll be home soon."

"Wonderful, Kate! You're amazing. Does Sheriff Roberts know?"

"I told him yesterday afternoon. While I was at Town Hall, Skip called him. He's giving Skip until Monday evening to get home and turn himself in."

"Alan is a good sheriff, but he tends to see everything in black and white. I hope he isn't too rough on poor Skip." Livvy sighed. "Still no idea who took the coin?"

"Oh, I have some ideas, but nothing I can prove. I still want to talk to Gertie Crowe. I keep leaving her messages, but I can't get ahold of her."

"Gertie hates telephones. She might have seen something, but I'm sure she told Alan everything she knows."

"Maybe. Or she might have missed some little detail." Kate didn't add that she had reason to suspect the cleaning lady.

"Yeah, and you'd be the one to figure it out. Well, Sherlock, I hope you do. In the meantime, I'd better get going. I have groceries in the car."

"Thanks for the flowers, Watson." Kate laughed and then gave Livvy a hug.

"You're welcome," Livvy said, returning Kate's hug. "You deserve it."

"I don't know about that, but I'm grateful," Kate said as she walked Livvy to the door.

Kate spotted the cards that she'd set aside when Dolores came. She carried them into the kitchen and was spreading them out on the table to write on and address when the doorbell rang. Sighing, she went to the door. Sheena stood there looking tired. Everyone seemed tired today.

"Hi, Kate. I just got off work. Is Tom finished?"

"I don't think so. Come in and wait for him. Would you like a cup of coffee?"

"No, thanks." She removed her coat and hung it on the coat tree.

Resigned that she wouldn't complete her cards that afternoon, Kate sat down with Sheena for a visit. The telephone rang. Kate excused herself and went into the kitchen to answer it. It was someone selling tickets to a benefit. Kate refused and returned to the living room.

It was like Grand Central Station at the Hanlon's that afternoon.

PAUL LOOKED AT HIS WORK CENTER. He smiled at Tom. "Very nice. It's just what I envisioned. Maybe better."

Tom looked pleased as he surveyed his work, but he didn't say anything. He began cleaning up, putting his tools away, and sweeping up their debris.

"We need to settle up," Paul said. "I owe you some money."

Tom nodded. "Could you . . . ah, would you give me a recommendation?"

Paul stopped picking up his things and looked at Tom.

Tom looked down at his shoes, then rocked back on his heels. He glanced up, giving Paul a sidewise look. "Just in case I need it," he said.

"I'd be happy to recommend the quality of your work, Tom—"

"Good. Thanks, Preach."

"But . . . I can't recommend your reliability. If someone asks, I'll have to be honest."

Tom pursed his lips and nodded. "Fair enough."

"I'll be right back." Paul went to his study and took out the money he'd set aside for his workbench project. He made a note on the project form that he'd had Tom sign before.

On a whim, he grabbed an unused men's study Bible off his bookshelf. He often kept extra Bibles on hand to give away. He took a moment to write a note in the front of it, then returned to the garage.

"I tried to keep track of the hours you were here," he said. He handed Tom the project form he'd created and a pen. "If you'd take a look and make sure I'm paying you the right amount, then sign this." Paul handed him the cash.

Tom looked at Paul's figures and frowned. "I know there was some extra time in there for lunches and stuff. You don't have to pay me for that," he said, holding out the money.

Paul nodded. "Tell you what. I have a gift for you. I wrote some passages for you to look up. You can keep all the money. All I ask is that you look up these references." He handed Tom the Bible.

Tom hesitated a moment, then reached out and took it. "Least I can do," he muttered. He scrawled his name on Paul's form, then folded the money without counting it and shoved it in his pocket.

Tom opened the door to the house and called Sheena. She told Kate good-bye, grabbed her coat and bag, and left. Paul watched them pull out of the driveway.

"Hey, Katie, come see my workbench," he called into the house.

She appeared in a moment. When she stepped into the garage, he flipped on the track light, illuminating his new work area.

"Wow." She examined every shelf and corner, smoothing her hand across the top. "He's slow, but he did a very professional job." She glanced over her shoulder. "What do *you* think? Is it what you wanted?"

"Yes. It's more than I envisioned. Honestly, he did a lot more for me than I did for him, even though I paid him well. I got a useful asset. I tried to give him some tools to help him succeed, but I'm afraid I failed."

"I know how you feel. I feel the same way about Sheena. I just keep praying something will click in their minds and make a difference. Maybe not today, but in God's timing."

"Yes. He won't delay. I believe that." The corner of his mouth turned up on one side. "Sure would be nice to see it in my lifetime."

PAUL CHANGED INTO WORK CLOTHES after church on Sunday. He couldn't wait to arrange his tools in his new work space. Kate had said she wanted to finish her Valentine projects and send the cards, so he helped clean up after a light lunch and

then left her at the kitchen table, where she'd set up her projects, gel pens, stamps, stickers, and a box of Valentine cards.

Standing in front of the workbench and shelves, armed
with a diagram he'd sketched to organize his work area, he
rubbed his hands together with glee. *What first?*

He carried the cardboard boxes of tools, some of which
he'd never unpacked from their move, and stacked them next
to the workbench.

He laid out the contents of the first box, carefully unwrap-
ping each tool: a rasp, two files, several chisels in various
widths, a folding ruler, a square, and a pair of calipers. These
deserved a place where they could be admired. He made room
for them on the magnetic strip and put them next to his com-
mon tools.

His father, who had worked hard all his life as a cement-
plant worker, would have loved a workbench like this. Paul's
older brother should have inherited these tools, but he'd died
in Vietnam, and so the tools had gone to Paul, the only surviv-
ing son. They weren't expensive tools, but they were priceless.
And reliable, as he'd tried to tell Tom.

Paul put his father's hand drill and a few larger woodworking tools in the tool chest beneath the workbench. The cardboard boxes were empty. The workbench was neat and clean.

He stepped back to admire the finished, furnished work
center. It was all he'd wanted. He broke down the boxes and
stacked them by the recycle bins, swept the area, then went
inside.

He poured himself a cup of coffee, then looked over at
Kate.

"Can I get you a coffee refill?" he asked.

"Yes, thanks." She held up her empty mug. "Are you finished arranging your tools already?"

"Yes, and it looks great."

"I bet it does. You're fast," she said. "I've only done a fourth of my list."

"That's because you write an epistle on every card."

"True. So what project will you tackle first?"

"I saw a junior workbench I'd like to make for Ethan. The plans are in that project magazine I bought. I'll go find it and make a list of the supplies I need."

"And I'll finish these cards. I need to mail them tomorrow."

Paul started through the living room and remembered his father's coin collection, which he'd set inside the house the previous day. He went to the end table to retrieve it and put the coins away someplace safe. The box wasn't there. He looked around.

"Kate, did you put my dad's coins somewhere?" he called.

Kate came into the living room. "Coins? I didn't see them. Did you put them in here?"

"Yes. I set them on the table here yesterday. I was showing Tom a tool, and I set the coin box on the workbench, then accidentally knocked it off. The box cracked on top, and the coins spilled out. We picked them up, and I put them . . . there," he said, pointing to the table.

She frowned and looked around. "They must be here somewhere."

Kate picked up magazines and newspapers and even checked inside the piano bench. She stood in the middle of the room, looking around, shaking her head.

"I don't know. When was it? Was Sheena here?"

"No. Before that."

Kate rubbed her forehead. "This place was a revolving door yesterday. Livvy came by. Dolores and her friend Trixie were here. Someone came by while I was talking with Dolores. Trixie got the door. Whoever it was didn't stay, and I forgot to ask Trixie. Who else was here?"

"Tom. Sheena."

"All right. Someone must have moved them. Let's look everywhere."

"Right."

The two got to work, looking in every nook and cranny they could fathom, finally finishing their search in their bedroom.

Paul plunked down on the edge of the bed. "They're not here."

"Don't worry," Kate said. "They'll turn up. It was so confusing around here yesterday, somehow they got moved."

He ran his fingers through his hair. "I can't imagine where they are, but I can't believe anyone would take them."

"Neither can I," Kate said. "I'm sure there's a perfectly logical explanation."

Chapter Twenty-Two

Kate sat at the table with her unfinished Valentines, wanting to complete her task but unable to concentrate. She kept trying to think where the coins might be. The phone rang. She got up and answered it.

"Kate, it's Dolores. Skip's home!"

"What? Already? I didn't expect him until tomorrow."

"He took a bus and got in early this morning. He called me from the bus station. I dropped him off at his apartment, 'cause he said he needed to sleep for a while. He looks exhausted, but he says he's all right."

"Is he there now?"

"No. He's on his way to your house."

"How are you holding up?"

"I'm fine. Kate, he won't talk to me about where he's been. I know you found him, so you must know where he was, but why did he leave? I don't understand any of this. I guess I should be thankful that at least he's home."

"I'll talk to him and encourage him to tell you. You know he has to go report to the sheriff."

"Yes, and he'll arrest Skip."

"I'm afraid so. I hope Skip has a satisfactory explanation and can shed some light on the missing coin. By the way, Dolores, I know you have a lot on your mind, but I just have a quick question for you. When you were here yesterday, did you happen to see an old wooden box with a cracked lid in the living room? We've misplaced it and can't find it. I'm assuming someone who was here might have moved it."

"No. Sorry, Kate. I don't remember seeing anything. I hope it wasn't something important."

"Just some old collectibles from Paul's dad. It'll turn up, I'm sure. Is Trixie there? Maybe she moved them."

"She's taking a nap. Do you want me to wake her?"

"No. Let her sleep. I can talk to her later. Thanks, Dolores." She didn't want to concern Dolores more, so she didn't mention they were coins.

Kate found Paul in his study going through a woodworking magazine. He looked up when she entered his office. She could tell by his distracted look that he was having trouble concentrating too.

"Skip's home. I just had a call from Dolores."

Paul whistled. "That was fast."

"I'll say. He's on his way here."

"Are you going to call the sheriff?"

"No. Skip needs to be the one to do that."

SKIP ACCEPTED a mug of coffee and sat in a chair across from Kate and Paul in the living room.

"I'm sorry my sudden trip left everything in such a mess. It's been so quiet around here, I figured I'd arranged for a replacement, and everything would be fine. I should have called the sheriff before I left, but it all happened so fast."

"What happened, Skip? Why did you tear out of here in such a hurry?" Kate asked.

Skip gave her a bleak look and sighed. "I can't tell you that. At least not yet. I promised. It's nothing bad . . . at least not about me. I told you on the phone, and it's the truth, Missus Hanlon. I didn't take that coin."

"I know you were at Town Hall Thursday morning before you left, since you released Billy Hart. Did you notice if the coin was in the case that morning?"

"No. I didn't look. That coin's been there for years. Only time I think about it is when Gertie Crowe asks for the key to clean the inside of the case."

"Which she did Tuesday afternoon. The coin was seen in place late Wednesday afternoon, so it disappeared after that," Kate said. "I'd hoped to find someone who saw it after you left, Skip, but no luck so far."

"I can't believe anyone would think I took it. I called Sheriff Roberts and he wants to see me today. I said I'd meet him at Town Hall at three thirty. It's almost that now, so I guess I'd better go turn myself in."

"Would you like us to go with you?" Kate asked.

Skip looked relieved. "That'd be great. I didn't want to ask. You've already done so much to help me."

"We'll be glad to. Would you like us to pray with you before we go?" Paul offered.

"Yeah, I'd like that. Maybe coming from you, it might do some good," Skip said. He bowed his head.

Kate thought he looked a little like a man preparing for a guillotine. She bowed her head and added a silent, fervent prayer for help and strength to Paul's plea for Skip.

LATE THAT AFTERNOON, Kate felt completely drained as she and Paul walked up the sidewalk to Dolores' front door. Kate was glad Paul had come with her. Dolores knew her son had to face the sheriff eventually, but Kate had hoped it wouldn't come to an actual arrest.

Dolores answered the door. Seeing them both, she frowned.

"It's bad news, isn't it? Has he been arrested?" she asked as soon as they stepped inside and closed the door.

"I'm afraid so. We went with him to meet the sheriff. Skip's statement didn't help him. He won't say why he left."

"I don't understand him. I've got to go talk to him." She opened a closet and grabbed a jacket and her purse.

"We'll take you," Paul said.

Tears rushed into her eyes. She nodded. "Thank you. I'll tell . . ."

Trixie came out of the kitchen just then and saw Dolores slip on her coat. "What's wrong? Where are you going?"

"Kate and Pastor Paul are taking me to Town Hall. Skip's been arrested."

"Oh dear." Trixie's face registered alarm. She wrung her hands together. "I'll . . . I'd better wait here for you. I'd just be in the way. Don't worry, Dee. It's all a misunderstanding. Didn't you say all they have is a circumstantial case, Kate?"

"As far as I know, there's no evidence to prove Skip took the coin."

Paul opened the door and held the screen open for Dolores.

"It'll be all right," Trixie said, consoling Dolores.

Kate's feelings echoed Trixie's bleak expression.

Paul smiled reassuringly in Trixie's direction as Kate followed Dolores out the door.

Dolores was silent the few minutes of the drive.

They didn't see anyone they knew outside Town Hall. A couple strolled along the sidewalk all bundled up, walking their dog. They were deep in conversation and didn't look up. Paul and Kate walked on either side of Dolores up the sidewalk and steep steps to Town Hall and the deputy's office. The old brick building appeared more austere than usual as their footsteps echoed down the hall.

The sheriff was gone. Deputy Martin sat behind Skip's desk, typing something into the computer. Kate watched Dolores pull herself together, standing straight and steeling her expression as she approached the office. Hugh looked up as they entered the small office. He stood.

"Mrs. Spencer," he said.

"I came to see my son," Dolores said.

"Of course. Just a moment." He took the keys to the jail cells off the hook in back of the door and unlocked the double doors.

Kate had visited prisoners behind those doors before. So had Paul. She imagined Dolores had seen the cells too, but with her son in uniform, showing his mother where he worked. *Please Lord, give Dolores strength to face the pain of seeing her son on the other side of those bars*, Kate prayed silently.

Hugh returned. "He'll see you if you want to follow me ma'am," he said.

Dolores held her head high as she followed the deputy, then disappeared inside the small jail. Kate glanced at Paul. He was frowning. He caught her gaze and reached for her hand, giving her his strength as if he read her thoughts and the despair she felt for Dolores and Skip.

Paul motioned toward two metal chairs against the wall in the deputy's office. "We might as well sit and wait."

Kate nodded and took a seat. She fidgeted with the edge of her cardigan sweater, fastening and unfastening the last button.

Paul nudged her shoulder. She looked up. At his raised eyebrow, her hand stilled. She sighed. The deputy came back and sat behind the desk, but he didn't say anything. He resumed his work.

Fifteen minutes later, Dolores came back. Her shoulders drooped under the weight of her distress. Resignation had replaced the determination on her face.

"He told me not to arrange bail," she said. "May I bring him dinner?" she asked the deputy.

"I don't see any reason why he couldn't have a homemade meal."

"Thank you. I'll bring it by in an hour. I suppose you have to stay here too."

"Yes, ma'am. We won't leave him alone."

"Good. I'll bring dinner for you too."

"You don't have to do that ma'am."

"I know. I want to. I'll be back in an hour," she said. She turned to Paul and Kate. "I'm ready to leave."

They walked on either side of Dolores for support as they left the building. It was getting dark. The streetlights had come on.

"Skip said you found him in Florida because of his truck. I can't believe he went tearing off just to get someone to work on that junk heap," Dolores said as they walked down the steps. "And he didn't even bring it back. It makes no sense. He said he had to help a friend, but he can't—or won't—say who. He's kept track of all his friends from grammar school clear through college. He's so loyal. I told him this can't be much of a friend if he'll let Skip go to jail rather than give him an alibi."

Three teenage boys were clowning around, hitting each other with wet snowballs in front of Town Hall. Otherwise, the streets were empty.

"Funny how life goes on, no matter what happens," Dolores said as they got into the car. "I wonder if life will ever seem normal to me again . . ."

Kate didn't have an answer. What was normal anyway? Life constantly changed.

"You've been through hardship before," Paul said. "You lost your husband, and you still raised a fine young man. You found a new normal. How did you do that?"

Dolores smiled halfheartedly. "Kickin' and screamin'," she said. "I was younger then, but guess that's how I'll handle this too."

They reached Dolores' house. She insisted she would be fine and said good-bye to them at the curb. She had a meal to prepare for Skip and the deputy. Her shoulders were squared, and her posture straight as she marched up the sidewalk to her front door.

"I'm afraid Skip's going to need a good lawyer," Kate said as they drove away. "His story about helping a friend didn't impress Sheriff Roberts."

"Obviously Skip's protecting someone, so he may refuse to talk out of loyalty," Paul said.

"Probably misplaced in this case. I hope he can see that, for his mother's sake if nothing else."

Chapter Twenty-Three

K ate woke earlier than usual Monday morning and couldn't go back to sleep. A single word was floating around in her mind. *Truth*. Yes, that's what she needed to discover. But the word wouldn't go away. Finally she gave up and rose.

It was still dark outside. The house was cold. Wrapping herself in her robe, she went through her morning routine, grinding and making coffee, starting a fire in the fireplace, then settling in front of it with her Bible and coffee mug.

She'd told Paul her plans to visit Skip at the jail and try to convince him to tell her where he'd been. They'd prayed together before bedtime, and she'd slept, clinging to God's promise that he would not delay. She didn't intend to tell Skip that, however. For him, time was of the essence.

Kate was reading in Galatians. It talked about being free from the Law. Skip wasn't free, at least not from the laws of Tennessee.

After her devotional time, she got dressed, then made a run to the post office to mail her Valentines. When she got back to the house, Tom was there, just backing out of the driveway.

She waved at him, but he ignored her and squealed his tires as he tore away.

Paul was still home. He came out of his study when Kate entered from the garage.

"What did Tom want?" she asked.

Paul looked disturbed. "He came to return a tool that had gotten mixed in with his tools." Paul ran his hand through his hair.

"Oh." Kate frowned. "He seemed angry."

Paul sighed. "He was. We had a . . . misunderstanding. I told him we couldn't find the coins and asked him if he'd moved them. He . . . he assumed I was accusing him of stealing them. I guess I didn't deny that quickly enough. He got mad and said he'd been trying to do me a favor and look where it got him. He said he'd thought we were different than his father and all the men he'd worked for."

"Oh dear. Do *you* think he took your dad's coins?"

Kate had wondered the same thing. If he'd taken their coins, he could have taken the Copper Mill coin. Sheena said they'd toured Town Hall, and the mayor had told them about the coin's value when they first moved to town. That wasn't cause for suspicion in itself, but she couldn't rule them out either.

Paul walked to his study doorway, then turned around. "No. Well . . . I don't know. The thought had crossed my mind. I don't want to think that, but he was here. He saw the coins and knew I'd put them in the house. What else should I think?"

"Oh, Paul." Kate went to him and gave him a hug, just holding him for a few moments. "We didn't do very well with Tom and Sheena, did we?"

"I blew it. I'm sorry, Kate."

"Me too. I'd hoped we could give them some positive encouragement and direction. Still, I just don't see them taking the coins. Maybe someday we'll get another chance with them."

"I hope so."

KATE WALKED THROUGH the heavy doors into the small two-celled jail facility and heard the thud as the doors closed. Her chest constricted, as if there wasn't enough oxygen. The artificial light cast a yellowed, sickly hue on everything. The windowless walls with their chipped, faded paint closed in on her. The meager facilities were barely adequate for a short-term incarceration. Most prisoners who stayed overnight were either moved or released, but the county jail was often overcrowded.

The first cell was empty. Skip sat on the bunk in the second cell. The Skip that Kate knew—the deputy with his back straight in a proud stance—was slumped over in a posture of utter defeat. When he looked up, the dark circles and bags beneath his eyes and the pallor of his pale, freckled complexion gave him a haunted appearance. He rose but didn't look directly at her.

"Hi," Kate said. She held out a small paper sack. "I brought you some cookies." The bars were just wide enough to pass the sack through to him.

"Thanks." He stood until she pulled a folding chair over and sat down.

He sat on the bunk, holding the cookies and looking at the floor.

"How are you?" Kate asked.

He shrugged. "Okay. Mom brought in breakfast. I told her it's not necessary, but she insisted."

"She has to do something, and right now, it's the only thing she can think to do."

"I don't like her coming in here."

"Then we need to get you out. Have you told the sheriff why you left and who you were with so you can establish an alibi?"

"Alibi?" He let out a short huff. "Wouldn't do any good."

"It might."

"I thought about the coin," Skip said, his eyes trained on the ground, "and I'm sure it was there when I left."

Kate raised her eyebrows. "You told me you didn't look. So what makes you so certain it was there?"

"The key was hanging on the hook, same as it had been. The jail keys were on top. I'd gone in to talk to my prisoner. The key was in the same place Thursday morning when I went to release him. Mom told me you got that straightened out for me. I appreciate it."

"The missing coin may not have anything to do with your absence, but you can see how it looks incriminating, can't you?"

"Yeah." He sighed. "I thought people knew me better than that."

"You could clear that up."

His jaw clenched. After a long silence, it became obvious he didn't intend to reveal his secret.

"Skip, I've watched what this has done to your mother since you left. She believes in you. She's defended you. She's worried and prayed for you. I'm sure people don't mean to be cruel, but they talk."

Skip hit the wall with his fist, startling her. "That's not right," he said through gritted teeth.

Kate planted her hands on her hips and gave him her best glare. She wanted to grab him by the shoulders and shake some sense into him, as she would feel about her own children when they dug in their heels. "No? Then make it right."

"I can't. I promised my friend. There's a good reason."

"Skip, you had to swear an oath when you became a deputy, didn't you?"

"Yes, ma'am."

"I suppose you took it seriously."

He straightened. "Very seriously."

"Well, then, you have just as much loyalty to your badge. You are a deputy, Skip. You're also your mother's son. You can't separate your actions from affecting both."

Skip looked miserable. "I don't want to hurt anyone."

"I believe that. Paul and I have been praying for you since I saw you Thursday morning driving away in your old truck. I knew something was wrong. Then I discovered the missing coin. I've been trying to find the thief. You're not the only suspect, but I can't find proof of the exact time it disappeared or who took it. Without that, you're the most likely suspect."

Skip squirmed. He leaned his elbows on his knees and rested his chin on his hands, looking down.

Kate couldn't tell if he was listening or ignoring her. What could she say to get through to him? *Help me, Lord. Don't let him ruin his life over some misguided loyalty.*

"You've put your trust and allegiance in the law. Are you going to disobey the law and your boss?"

"What about loyalty to my friends," he asked, his gaze bleak and troubled.

"Loyalty is a good thing, Skip, but not when one loyalty betrays another. If you're protecting someone by helping him hide something, that is a lie, and lies lead to destruction. That's why God puts so much weight on the truth."

Skip covered his face with his hands. "What a mess. I don't know what to do."

"The very fact that you call it a mess should tell you what to do. I know you would advise someone you caught breaking the law to tell the truth. Don't you think you should follow your own advice?"

He nodded his head, still looking down. He raked his fingers through his hair. "I went to see my friend Gary Davenport."

"Trixie's son?"

"Yeah. I called him that morning to talk about a fishing tournament. H-h-he needed my help. He sent his mom up here because they discovered a gas leak at their house. It was giving them both headaches. But he'd had an accident in his welding shop before that and hurt his back, and he'd been taking pain pills. Lots of pain pills. He got hooked. He'd been sitting there staring at a bottle of pills when I called. He was d-desperate."

Skip's refusal to explain his trip began to make sense. "And he doesn't want his mother to know."

He looked up at that. "I can't blame him. I wouldn't want my mom to know if I was on drugs. He thought he could control it, but then the headaches started. It was affecting his work. He was afraid he'd lose his business if people found out.

He needed to fix the gas leak, but he needed to go to a rehab center, and he couldn't afford it or take the time."

"So you withdrew all your savings and went tearing down to Alabama to help him. What was in Florida?"

His head shot up. "How'd you know about my savings?"

Kate smiled. "I may not have found the thief, but I learned a lot."

"That's where the rehab center is. So everyone knows I took my money out. And the coin disappeared when I left. No wonder the sheriff thinks I took it."

"It doesn't look good."

"Honest, Missus Hanlon. I didn't take it."

"Honest, Skip, I believe you. I want to prove it and clear your name. Knowing why you went helps. You're going to have to tell the sheriff and your mother."

"Proving where I went won't prove I didn't steal the coin. I have a hearing at the courthouse in Pine Ridge this afternoon at three. The judge will probably turn it over to a grand jury to decide. I don't want Mrs. Davenport to know. I promised Gary. Besides, it'd only hurt her. Mom wouldn't want that either. I'll tell her after Mrs. Davenport leaves."

"I think she's leaving tomorrow."

"Yeah. While Gary was in detox, they wouldn't let him have visitors for the first few days, so I went back and fixed his gas leak. The house is ready. He was supposed to get out yesterday afternoon. I was going to wait to come home until I made sure he's all right."

"You came home on a bus. Did your truck break down? Or is it still in the body shop?"

"It got me there all right, but it was running rough. I heard about a guy who restores classic cars in his garage."

"Is that the one Jayme Johnson recommended?"

"You tracked her too?" he asked, giving her an incredulous look.

"Wasn't hard," Kate said.

Skip shook his head. "Yeah, I took it there to see what it'd take to restore it. It was going to cost more than it's worth. Besides, I used the money I'd saved to help pay for Gary's rehab. His insurance didn't cover it all. He'll pay me back, but it'll take a while. So the guy bought the truck for parts. I didn't get much for it. I'll have to save up to get another one." Skip shook his head. "'Course I won't have a job now. I messed up, didn't I?"

"With the best of intentions. I don't know if we can untangle all of this, Skip, but God knows. I've got a whole list of character witnesses for you. Maybe that will help. My best advice is tell the whole truth."

"Thanks, Missus Hanlon. Especially for being a friend to my mom. She doesn't deserve to be hurt by my actions."

Chapter Twenty-Four

As Kate left the jail area, she spotted a mop bucket down by the community room. She hurried down the hall. Gertie Crowe grabbed the mop and started washing the floor just as Kate got near her.

"Gertie, I've been wanting to talk to you," Kate said.

Gertie looked over her shoulder but didn't stop swinging her mop. "Yeah, I know."

"I wanted to ask you about Skip Spencer."

"I already told the sheriff what I know." She turned back to her task, cutting Kate off.

Kate couldn't help wondering why Gertie was so reluctant to talk to her. "Don't you want to help clear an innocent man? Please, I know you've been through this with the sheriff, but sometimes a woman notices things a man might miss."

"*Ha*. You ain't just whistlin' 'Dixie.' Women leave things a lot cleaner than the men around here. I got a whole sack of trash from the men that used the big room last night. Couldn't get in to clean up until this morning cause of their doings.

Couldn't leave it until tomorrow. Threw my whole schedule off. I can't be wasting time talking. I've got another job waiting."

"I know you're really busy. I won't take much of your time. Could you talk to me while you work?"

"What do you want to know?" She swiped the mop close to Kate's feet. Kate moved back.

"I know you got the display-case key from Deputy Spencer so you could clean the glass a couple of days before the coin disappeared. I heard that you noticed he was particularly interested in the coin or the display case or something. You know this building better than anyone else. I just wondered what you observed."

Gertie stopped mopping and turned to Kate. She leaned on her mop. "That boy was struttin' around here like he owned the place. He watched me clean the glass." She narrowed her eyes. "I can't abide someone lookin' over my shoulder like they're lookin' to make sure I don't miss a speck, like the mayor's wife and Clara Briddle. At least Lucy Mae isn't here when I'm workin', but that Clara is a busybody. Nobody bothered me much until she stuck her nose in here."

"Does Deputy Spencer always watch you like that?"

"No. He usually minds his business and lets me mind mine. Sometimes he even holds the door for me. I guess that's why I was surprised. I finished and locked the glass and handed him the key. He stood there just staring at the coin and polishing that key. He was hatching up a plan, seems to me. He's like that, you know." She gave a humorless chuckle. "Gets some hair-brained idea in his head and goes off and does something crazy. That's happened more than once. I've heard the sheriff reading him the riot act and grounding him to that desk in there."

"Skip might be impulsive, but that doesn't make him a thief."

Gertie winced. She stood there holding her mop for a moment, her lips pursed. Kate watched Gertie's expression change from defensive to distressed. She looked at Kate, her eyes begging Kate for something. Understanding?

"It was mighty nice of you to bring a basket of food by my place. Why'd you do it?"

"Clara told me you didn't make it to work last Tuesday. I thought you might be sick."

Gertie let out a deep sigh. "I wasn't sick. I just changed my hours. You kept hounding me, and I didn't want to talk to you."

"Why not, Gertie? What are you hiding?"

Gertie stared at her for a moment. Her eyes filled with tears. She cleared her throat. "Skip didn't take that coin, although he could have. I'm afraid . . ." Gertie squared her shoulders. "I'm pretty sure my daughter took the coin. She and my grandson are living with me now, you know. She's in a heap of financial trouble with her ex-husband running up all kinds of bills.

"I saw her looking at the coin when I came by here that Wednesday morning. I could just see it in her eyes. And she's been real quiet and secretive since then." Gertie choked up, her voice barely above a hoarse whisper. "She's not a bad girl, but she's made some bad choices. I thought coming here, she'd get her life straightened out."

Gertie shook her head. "If she goes to jail, I can't take care of Michael. I have to work. Besides, I can't keep up with him."

"The coin didn't disappear until after four o'clock Wednesday afternoon. Lucy Mae positively saw it then."

"She did?" Gertie's eyes grew big. "But then Prissy couldn't have taken it. She took Michael and went to visit a friend in Pine Ridge that afternoon, and she spent the night. She didn't come home until Saturday morning. I thought . . . I thought she went to hock the coin or something. I . . ." Tears started streaming down Gertie's face.

Kate steered her into the women's bathroom. Gertie went along without resistance.

"I thought my girl did something terrible and took that coin. And here, all along, I was wrong."

Kate could see the relief, the weight of guilt, fall off Gertie's shoulders.

"But that means Skip might really have taken it," Gertie said. "I was hoping, since he's a deputy and there wasn't any real proof, that he'd get off. I really did see him standing there staring at it. Now what will happen to him?"

"I don't know," Kate said. "What makes you think he was looking at the coin and not reading one of the articles?"

"He said the coin meant a lot to the town."

"He said that to you?"

"No. He wasn't talking to me. He had a lady with him."

Kate couldn't recall ever seeing Skip with a girl, but he was single and attractive in a friendly sort of manner. "A girlfriend?"

"No, no. This woman was old enough to be his mother."

"Do you know his mother?"

"Sure do. I've been around here a long time, you know. She used to work in one of my buildings. This wasn't Dolores Spencer. No, sir. I didn't recognize this lady, but she talked like she'd been here before. She said things hadn't changed much. He was showing off where he worked. That's all. I got my mop bucket and left after that. He was still standing there, rubbing on that key as if I'd left fingerprints on it and staring at that coin."

"Thank you, Gertie. That could be a vital piece of the puzzle." The woman with Skip had to be Trixie, she thought.

"Not likely," Gertie said. "The woman wasn't paying any attention to it. Just Skip was looking at it. Tell you what, though. Now I know it wasn't my Prissy, I'll do anything I can to help you find the real thief."

Kate left Gertie in the ladies' restroom and returned to the deputy's office to see Skip, who was surprised to see her again so quickly.

"Before you left town, did you bring Mrs. Davenport down here to see your office?" Kate asked.

"We stopped by here Tuesday afternoon. I took her all over town. She hadn't been here for years. Why?"

"I just wondered. The cleaning lady saw you staring at the coin after she cleaned the cabinet and gave the key back to you. I just saw her, and she mentioned that a woman was with you. Since she didn't recognize her, I assumed it was Trixie. I just wondered if she could help clear you."

"I don't see how. I came back in Thursday morning before I left. That's when I released Billy."

"So why were you staring at the coin that afternoon?"

"Mrs. Davenport was telling me about when the mine closed. I guess it was really a tough time around here. I was pretty young, so it didn't affect me too much. It just got me thinking. Then she wanted to go have an ice cream. She remembered a special sundae Mrs. Blount used to make. So I treated her to an ice cream sundae. Then we went back to the house, and mom had a big dinner, but we were both full. We had to eat it anyway."

Skip grinned at the memory. Kate grinned too. It was good to see him smile.

KATE SAT AT THE KITCHEN TABLE with her notepad and a cup of coffee. *Write down the revelation and make it plain. . . . It speaks of the end and will not prove false. Though it linger, wait for it; it will certainly come and will not delay,* Kate recalled, remembering the Bible passage Paul had quoted to her from Habakkuk.

She crossed Gertie and Prissy off her list of suspects, then jotted down the account Gertie had given her. From Gertie's point of view, Kate could see how the cleaning lady had been puzzled by Skip's preoccupation with the coin. Kate hadn't realized its full value until she'd started researching it. It didn't look particularly valuable.

So where did that leave her?

Kate took her notes and went over each item. As she did, she got up and walked around.

Activity helped her think. Kate went out to the garage to wash Paul's work clothes. She checked the pockets and shook the trousers out. He'd clearly tried to brush off the dirt on the knee. She started to spray the smudge, then stopped. It didn't look like dirt. She touched it. A fine, light dust clung to her finger. She sniffed it. Not sawdust. Not dirt. Where had he been recently? They'd been looking for the box of coins.

Kate went back inside, got down on her hands and knees,

and ran her hands over the green shag carpet beneath the table where Paul had set the coins. She raised her hand and looked at it. A sheen of light powder stuck to her fingers. In a flash of realization, Kate knew just what that meant.

Chapter Twenty-Five

Dolores wore a brown-smeared bib apron over her denim pants and long-sleeved top. Her hair was frizzed as if she'd been in a steam room. She waved a wooden spoon at Kate from the kitchen doorway when Trixie let Kate into the house on Monday afternoon.

"Be right there," Dolores called out. "Want coffee?"

"No, thanks. I'm good," Kate hollered back. She followed Trixie to the living room. "How are you, Trixie? I heard you're leaving tomorrow. You ready to get back to your normal routine?"

"Yes. I can't wait to get home. The house is ready. My son needs me. He doesn't eat properly if I'm not there to fix meals, you know."

"Oh yes. I have a son too," Kate said. "Before he got married, I got on his case a lot about his diet. He lived on fast food most of the time."

Trixie sighed. "Do we ever quit worrying about our children?"

"I know I don't," Kate said.

Dolores came in and sat down. She'd removed her apron. "I was cooking dinner and snacks for Skip and Hugh...er ...Deputy Martin. He's been so nice." She frowned. "I could just shoot Sheriff Roberts, though. Not literally, of course. I tried to talk to him last night. He listened, and he sympathized with me, but he said he can't ignore the evidence."

"They don't have any evidence. They can't do anything to Skip without proof," Trixie said. "He'll be out of there in no time."

"I'm afraid that's not true," Kate said. "If a grand jury believes the circumstantial evidence is condemning enough, he will go to trial." She took a short pause. "But I did have a thought that might help Skip's case..."

Dolores perked up. "What?"

"I was hoping you might have seen something, Trixie?"

Trixie looked stunned. "Me? Why would I know something?"

"Well, I thought since Skip took you to see his office and Town Hall before he left, maybe you noticed something in the building. Gertie, the cleaning lady, said Skip was staring at the coin and talking to you."

"Oh, well, he showed me around. I hadn't been here for years, you know. He thought I'd like to see how things had changed."

"You didn't tell me that, Trixie," Dolores said.

"Well, it wasn't important. We just stopped there because he had to do something. He showed me around town, and we were on our way to the store to run an errand for you, Dee."

"And did you?" Kate asked.

"Yes. We went to the Mercantile."

"*Hmm*." Kate sighed. "That's too bad. I was hoping you might have noticed something. Has the town changed much? I saw you talking with Renee Lambert and others at church. Were you able to visit friends and relive old memories?"

"Not really. If it weren't for Dee, I'd never come back," Trixie said. "I couldn't get away from here too soon after Gary graduated. It was his friends who were here, not mine. Copper Mill never felt like home to me."

"Trixie's husband worked for the mines," Dolores said. "Our husbands worked together. When the mines shut down, they all lost their jobs. It was hard times. We were fortunate. My husband had his electrical license, so he found work, but we struggled. I worked at the post office, so we got by."

"Hard times for the miners," Trixie said. "Not the owners. They lived in the city. They weren't stuck with worthless houses and no jobs. Burt should have gotten disability. He got hurt working in the mine, but he never got a cent. He had so much pain, he couldn't work."

Trixie shook her head. "Weren't any jobs anyways. I had to get work in Pine Ridge at the nursing home. Burt gave up. He finally went looking for work elsewhere. He was going to send for us when he got settled in a job. Gary was ten. We never heard from him until one day several years later, I got a notice that he'd died out west. Didn't leave a cent. Just more bills."

"How sad for you and your son," Kate said.

"Yes, well, that's water under the bridge," Trixie said. "Copper Mill is still a dead-end town, if you ask me. Oh, business is better, but not like when the mines were running."

"Were you surprised by any changes when Skip showed you around?" Kate asked again.

"Well, they've painted Town Hall and fixed it up. Skip's real proud of his office there. He showed me the jail and all."

"With all the hardships you endured in Copper Mill, that display case must have brought back bad memories, with the articles and pictures about the mine and all. As a newcomer, it all fascinated me."

"Hmmph," Trixie huffed. Her mouth turned down, and her eyes took on a hard glare. "There wasn't anything glamorous about those mines, was there, Dee? They should show all the men with miner's lung and disabilities from injuries and the miserable working conditions."

"It must have been hard to look at that shiny copper coin," Kate said. "It glamorized the mining industry and showed the wealth that was gained by some. Not at all the way you remembered, was it?"

"That's for sure. The mines never gave us a thing."

"Is that why you exchanged the coin for a car-wash token?" Dolores gasped.

Trixie's gaze turned wary. "What? . . . I didn't . . ."

"You didn't do it when you were with Skip. You went back Thursday when he wasn't there."

"Trixie?" Dolores stared at her friend. "You did go to town without me Thursday morning. You said you had to mail something."

Trixie's countenance paled, and she clutched her hands across her chest. She turned to Dolores, her eyes pleading for understanding. "I didn't . . . I didn't mean to. Honest. I never even thought about it. I stopped by to see Skip and ask him to call Gary. I'm so worried about him."

"You told me he has headaches, but that should be better since he discovered the gas leak."

"No, it's more than that. I'm afraid . . . He's just not right. Something's wrong with him. Ever since he got hurt. Like his father."

Trixie drew a shaky breath. Her eyes filled with tears, and she seemed to shrink into herself. "I'm so sorry, Dee. I didn't mean to hurt you or Skip. Gary's acting like Burt when he started drinking all the time. You remember. He won't go to the doctor. He said he couldn't afford it. Just like Burt. He couldn't afford to get help."

Trixie's face twisted with anguish as she began to sob. She reached out her hands toward Dolores. "I'm afraid. I don't want my son to end up like his father and leave me. I can't let that happen."

Dolores went to her friend and hugged her. "Trixie, it's all right. Skip can talk to him. He'll help. We'll help."

Kate watched the interplay between the two women. Dolores would have had the right to be furious with Trixie's betrayal, but instead, she reached out to give comfort. No wonder her son was so loyal.

"I'll return the coin," Trixie said between sobs. She wiped at her eyes. "I had that silly token in my purse that I'd picked up at a truck stop on the way here. Just a silly souvenir. It was so easy. No one was around. The office door was open, and Skip wasn't there. I took it, then I didn't know what to do with it. I thought I'd sell it after I get home and pay for Gary to get help."

She turned to Kate. "How did you know?"

"Your baby powder. It was on the floor in front of the display case when I discovered the coin was missing, although I didn't realize what it was at the time. I love the smell. It's so light and fresh and unmistakable. I didn't recognize it on you at first because there were always other scents around to confuse my senses. Today I found it in my carpet beneath where Paul set his father's coin collection. You took that too, didn't you, Trixie?"

"The powder had spilled in my purse. Some of it must have fallen out when I took out the token."

"And when you opened your big purse in my house next to the couch."

Trixie stared at Kate and nodded, beseeching Kate and Dolores with her red-rimmed eyes. "I carry a plastic bottle in my purse. The top came off while I was traveling. I tried to empty it out, but it's everywhere. When I put the coins in my purse, I dropped it and some fell out. I tried to cover it up. I didn't mean to steal, Dee. You've been so kind. I don't know what got into me. I'm so s-s-sorry."

How far would I go for my son? Kate wondered. She couldn't imagine being desperate enough to steal or lie or cheat.

"Get that coin, Trixie," Kate said. "We've got to take it back right now. We've got to get Skip out of that jail."

Dolores shook off her shock and stood up straight, like a soldier ready to do battle. "Yes. Right now."

Trixie blew her nose and stood. She shuffled down the hall, her steps slow, her shoulders slumped.

Dolores watched her go and shook her head. "I can't believe it. She let Skip go to jail . . . I don't know what'll happen to her, but my son needs to be free, and not a moment to waste.

We've got to get there before he goes to court. I'll just go turn off the chili."

She started toward the kitchen, then turned back to Kate with a smile. "I just realized I won't need to take the chili to the jail. Skip will be home for dinner."

Kate smiled.

"I can't thank you enough," Dolores said. "Will you come with us to the jail to free Skip?"

"I wouldn't miss it. I'll drive."

Chapter Twenty-Six

Trixie's shoulders drooped as she shuffled back to the living room carrying the cracked wooden box with the carved top. The outside of the box was dusty with baby powder. She held it out to Kate.

"I'm so sorry," she said, her eyes pleading for understanding. "It was sitting there, all cracked. I figured you didn't care much about it, and I needed it for Gary. I just took it and stuck it down in my bag. That was wrong. I knew it was wrong. I don't deserve your forgiveness, or Dee's or Skip's forgiveness, and I don't know if my son will forgive me. I've really made a mess, haven't I?"

Kate took the box and then reached for Trixie's hand. Dolores had disappeared into the bathroom. "Thank you. This belonged to Paul's father, so it means a lot to us. But we forgive you. I'm sure your son and Dolores and Skip will forgive you too, but first you need to clear Skip. Do you have the coin?"

"Yes. It's right here." She reached into her pocket and pulled out a tissue. The coin was wrapped in the tissue. "I have to go to the sheriff, don't I?"

"Yes."

"I'll have to confess to Gary too. He'll be so angry. And Dolores. She's my best friend. I wouldn't blame her if she hated me after this."

"She won't."

THEY REACHED TOWN HALL TOO LATE. The office was empty. Deputy Martin had already taken Skip to Pine Ridge for his hearing. Trixie balked at going to the courthouse, but Dolores took her by the arm and escorted her back to Kate's car.

Glancing in her mirror, Kate could see the dread in Trixie's face as they drove to Pine Ridge. Kate suspected that getting caught wasn't Trixie's main concern. She'd sought a way to help her son and to hang on to him, and now that hope was dashed. Trixie didn't know that Skip had already helped her son. Skip and Gary didn't know that Trixie had guessed her son had a problem. *Lord, what do I do?* The answer came, swift and sure. The words of Habakkuk came back to Kate.

> Then the Lord replied: "Write down the revelation and make it plain on tablets so that a herald may run with it. For the revelation awaits an appointed time; it speaks of the end and will not prove false. Though it linger, wait for it; it will certainly come and will not delay."

Their trip was about more than freeing Skip. She glanced at Trixie in the mirror again.

"Trixie, I talked to Skip this morning. He didn't want to tell you where he'd been, but you need to ask him to tell you the whole truth."

Trixie glanced forward at the mirror, her brow wrinkled. Out of the corner of her eye, Kate saw Dolores turn and stare at her. She looked so confused, Kate wanted to reach over and comfort her, but maybe Skip's story would help her understand, if he'd tell them.

The parking lot at the courthouse was full. Kate parked on the side street. It was three o'clock. The hearing had just begun.

Dried tears streaked paths down Trixie's face, caking her makeup. Her eyes were red and puffy. Dolores amazed Kate by putting her arm around Trixie's waist as if to comfort her as they walked toward the wide, steep steps leading up to the imposing antebellum building with its stately, white columns and tall, thin windows.

Kate loved the old building, but she imagined it looked intimidating to Trixie.

The courtroom was upstairs, at the end of a hallway. The heavy oak doors were closed. Kate pushed them open. A guard just inside looked at them, then stepped out of their way so they could enter, Kate in the lead, then Trixie, followed by Dolores.

"Mr. Spencer," the judge's voice boomed. "I didn't expect to see you in my courtroom as a defendant. Do you have an attorney, son?"

Skip struggled to stand. "No, sir. I . . . I can't afford one, Your Honor."

Kate could see handcuffs on his wrists. The sight made her sick. She wished Dolores didn't have to see it.

The judge frowned. "According to this . . ."—he lifted a page and looked at the document in front of him—"you're charged with several misdemeanors and a serious crime. I'm going to assign counsel." He motioned with his hand.

"That won't be necessary, Your Honor," Kate said, hurrying to the front. Her voice sounded louder than she'd intended. The sound seemed to ricochet off the heavily paneled walls.

"And who are you, ma'am?" the judge asked.

Kate glanced at Sheriff Roberts at the front of the room. He came toward her. "Your Honor, this is Kate Hanlon from Copper Mill." He turned to her. "What's this all about?" he whispered loudly, stopping in front of her.

"Skip didn't take the coin," Kate said.

"Then who did?"

"Trixie Davenport has it." She turned to Trixie, who looked like she might expire from fright at any moment. "It's all right, Trixie. Give the coin to the sheriff."

Trixie reached into her pocket and took out the tissue-wrapped coin. Wide-eyed and shaking, she handed it to the sheriff.

"Sheriff," the judge called from the bench. "What's going on?"

Sheriff Roberts turned to the judge. "Apparently we have the wrong suspect."

PAUL ENTERED THE LIVING ROOM and found Kate working in the kitchen when he came in from his office at church. She turned and smiled at him.

"Hi, honey." He crossed to his study to deposit the materials he needed to work on that evening. He saw the coin box as soon as he reached his desk.

"Where did you find this?" he asked, coming out of the study and crossing to the kitchen, carrying the cracked box. He gave her a kiss.

"Dolores' friend Trixie had the box. I visited them this afternoon."

Paul's eyes widened as he sat across from her. "Trixie had the coins? Why would she take them?"

"For the same reason Skip disappeared. Her son, Gary. Skip and Gary went to school together here in Copper Mill. Then Gary and Trixie moved away after he graduated."

Paul raised his eyebrows. He had counseled enough people over his thirty-plus years of ministry to know how complicated relationships could become and how emotions caused people to make illogical decisions and suffer terrible consequences.

"Let me guess," he said. "Gary was having some serious problem, and Skip went to help, and Trixie was desperate to help her son."

"Bingo!" Kate sat back and grinned at her husband. "I should have let you figure this one out."

"I guess Skip is now free? What will happen to Trixie?"

"I don't know. Skip isn't out of hot water, but all he has against him now is bad communication. All this could have been avoided if he'd taken enough time to make sure the sheriff knew what was happening."

"I imagine his job could be on the line."

"Very possible. I'm praying for leniency."

The phone rang as Paul stood. He went to answer it.

"This is Paul," he said. He listened for a moment. "Sure. Fifteen minutes is fine. I'll see you then." He hung up. "That was Tom. He's coming over to talk to me. Maybe we should say those prayers right now."

PAUL PULLED ON A COAT and went out to the garage, opened the overhead door, and then puttered around, waiting for Tom. He had no idea what to expect. He and Tom hadn't parted well that morning. Now knowing who took his coin collection, he owed Tom an apology. When he'd asked if Tom or Sheena had moved the coins, Tom had jumped on the defensive, taking the question as an accusation. Paul hadn't meant it that way, but he had wondered.

The van pulled into the driveway, and Tom got out. He strolled into the garage, a screwdriver in his hand.

"Hey, Preach. How're ya doing?"

"Good, Tom." He smiled and reached out his hand in welcome. Tom shook it.

"I found another of your tools in my tool bucket. I guess it's easy to misplace things. I didn't mean to walk off with it."

"Thanks. I hadn't missed it. Say, I'm sure enjoying my workbench. I got this project to make for my grandson."

He showed Tom a picture of a miniature workbench with a slide-out shelf for tools. He picked up a piece of soft pine that he'd bought for the little workbench.

"I'll sand it smooth with curved edges. What do you think?"

Tom fingered the wood. "He'll love it."

Tom handed Paul the wood, then put his hands in his back pockets and looked down at his boots. "I've been reading that Bible you gave me." He looked up at Paul. "There's a lot of good advice in there. Funny thing . . . My dad tried to tell me those things, and I thought he was just being critical." Tom's mouth curled up in a lopsided smile. "But maybe he was right."

"I'm sure your father would love to hear that from you."

"Yeah. Maybe I'll call him, but not until I get on my feet. I went and talked to Doug Campbell. Told him I'm a good carpenter but not a great employee, but I'd appreciate it if he'd give me a try."

Tom scratched his head. "Don't know why, but he hired me." He grinned. "I start tomorrow. Looks like he's got enough work to keep me on if I can show up on time every day. And I intend to do that. I returned the Xbox to the store and told Sheena to start looking for a new place to live. We should be able to save enough for a deposit and two months' rent pretty fast."

"Tom, that's wonderful. Hey, I'm sorry I came down on you a little hard this morning. I didn't mean to accuse you of taking my coins."

"That's all right. I deserved it. Did you find them?"

"Actually, they were returned to us this afternoon."

Tom's eyes widened. "Someone took them? I thought, you know, maybe you forgot where you put them."

Ouch, Paul thought. Apparently Tom saw him as old, bordering on senile.

"Yeah, someone took them. I'm not upset. The person is going through some tough times. But the coins were my father's, so I'm glad to have them back."

"That's what I like about you, Preach. You've got it all together in here," Tom said, thumping his fist over his heart.

"Thanks, Tom, but I don't have it all together, as you say.

I'm working on it. God's working on me, perfecting me all the time. I make mistakes and have problems just like everyone else."

"I hear that," Tom said. "I gotta pick Sheena up from work now. Good thing I got this job. This is her last day. Her boss said she doesn't need her no more."

"I'm sorry to hear that. Perhaps she can find another job."

"Naw. She's going to work on her jewelry. I'm going to support us now." He stood tall and smiled. "Thanks for everything, Preach. I'll see you later."

Paul gave Tom a small wave as the young man backed up a few steps, then turned and walked to his van.

"Thank you, Lord," Paul whispered.

AFTER PAUL LEFT FOR THE CHURCH Tuesday morning, Kate spent some time in the kitchen. At ten o'clock, the doorbell rang. She walked to the entry and glanced out the window next to the door. A sheriff's department SUV was parked in front of the house. A man in uniform stood at the door, but all she could see was a leg and an arm. She figured the sheriff would want a statement about Trixie to tie up loose ends. She opened the door.

Skip was standing there holding a tall milk-glass vase with a big red bow around it, filled with red carnations, white chrysanthemums, and sprigs of eucalyptus. He didn't smile, and he still looked tired, but he stood straight and tall, no longer weighed down by troubles.

"Skip! Please come in."

He opened the screen door and stepped inside. "These are for you," he said, handing her the flowers.

"Thank you. They're beautiful! Come sit down." She took the flowers and set them on the coffee table in front of the couch. Skip sat on the edge of an overstuffed chair. He removed his hat and held it in his hands.

Kate sat across from him. "You're back on the job. I'm so glad. What happened? How's your mother?" She wanted to ask about Trixie but didn't want to spoil the relief she saw on his face.

"Mom's fine." He looked down at his hands, which were working their way around the rim of his hat. He stopped and raised his eyes to Kate's. "She says I turned her hair gray these past couple of weeks. I don't doubt it. I don't know how she puts up with me."

"She loves you," Kate said.

"I know. She said you were her lifeline. I can't thank you enough. If it weren't for you, I'd still be sitting in that cell. I never want to be on that side of the bars again. It gave me a whole new perspective on things."

Skip sighed.

"I guess you know the sheriff almost fired me. He put me on six months' probation. He said a bunch of people stood up for me and asked him to reinstate me. Thanks to them, he reversed my suspension. I have to take the time I missed as vacation, so I'll miss my bass tournament, but that's okay."

He stood. "I'm just thankful I got my job back. In fact, I have to get back to work, but I just wanted to say thank you in person, outside of a jail cell."

"I'm very glad to hear you're back on duty, Skip. You belong in that uniform, serving and protecting Copper Mill."

"Yes, ma'am." He gave her a quick salute, then strode out the door.

He walked tall down the sidewalk to his SUV, looking every inch the deputy enforcing the law.

Sweet contentment filled Kate as she watched Skip drive away. Law and order had been restored to Copper Mill.

About the Author

SUNNI JEFFERS calls a small farm set in remote northeast Washington State home. She loves spending time with her granddaughters and watching out her office window as hawks and eagles soar, and elk, deer, bear, moose and the occasional buffalo stop by the hay fields and forest for a munch. Sunni writes full time and has won the Romance Writers of America Golden Heart, American Christian Fiction Writers Book of the Year and the Colorado Romance Writer's Award of Excellence.

A Note from the Editors

THIS ORIGINAL BOOK was created by the Books and Inspirational Media Division of Guideposts, the world's leading inspirational publisher. Founded in 1945 by Dr. Norman Vincent Peale and Ruth Stafford Peale, Guideposts helps people from all walks of life achieve their maximum personal and spiritual potential. Guideposts is committed to communicating positive, faith-filled principles for people everywhere to use in successful daily living.

Our publications include award-winning magazines such as *Guideposts* and *Angels on Earth*, best-selling books, and outreach services that demonstrate what can happen when faith and positive thinking are applied in day-to-day life.

For more information, visit us at www.guideposts.com, call (800) 431-2344 or write Guideposts, PO Box 5815, Harlan, Iowa 51593.